TEENS OF TOMORROW

STORIES OF NEAR AND FAR-FLUNG FUTURES

Edited by
Kell Cowley and K.C. Finn

Foreword by
Professor Scott Lankford

Odd Voice Out Publishing
Chester, UK
www.oddvoiceout.com
oddvoiceout@gmail.com

Ordering Information:
ISBN: 978-1-291-32842-4
Quantity sales. Special discounts are available on quantity
purchases by corporations, associations, and others. For
details, contact the publisher at the email address above.

Printed in the United Kingdom

Contents

Introduction
- pg 5 -

Foreword by Professor Scott Lankford
- pg 9 -

Our Top Ten Tales:

The Brief Death Of Aparna by Shreyas Muthusankar
- pg 15 -

Maasai Lights by Mary Ball Howkins
- pg 43 -

Eye Of The Beholder by Alec James
- pg 61 -

School Strike For Baby Hope by David Thorpe
- pg 91 -

Crimson Constellations by Abby Mayers and Melody Lumb
- pg 107 -

Swamp Reeds by Mary Ball Howkins
- pg 129 -

The Zebra Genus by A. Rose
- pg 143 -

Pax Park by Margaret Forze
- pg 155 -

What We Do Know How To Do by Anneliese Schultz
- pg 179 -

Being Lavender Blue by Hannah Ray
- pg 199 -

Bonus Tales from the OVO Archive:

True America by Kell Cowley
- pg 217 -

Reach Out And Touch Faith by K.C. Finn
- pg 241 -

INTRODUCTION

Like many, we began our 2020 with big plans and bold ambitions. In the previous eighteen months, we had devised and launched our own indie YA fiction label Odd Voice Out, we'd released four novels, appeared at literary festivals up and down the country, led creative writing workshops in schools and our community, and we were just putting the finishing touches on our first anthology collection celebrating diverse narrators. In the first few months of the new decade, we were focused on the future, but also anxious over growing global threats to our environment, our democracy and basic human rights.

So over drinks in a crowded English pub, we elected to make 'Teens of Tomorrow' the theme of our next short story contest, calling on YA writers to send us their takes on how young people will tackle the many challenges they face in the coming years. It was a prompt asking for imaginary visions of near and far-flung futures. Little did we realize that all our concepts of the future were about to be dramatically reshaped, with many of our creature comforts (like the very barroom around us) soon to be stripped away.

We were all aware of the virus emerging in the east. It wasn't an unforeseen crisis, just one we hoped would fizzle out fast like other spikes of new flus we'd seen in our lifetimes. We were in no way prepared for the total shutdown of our daily lives. As writers, one of our earliest reactions was to assume that we were the lucky ones, the people who had the necessary coping mechanisms built into our reclusive natures. Escaping the outside world and locking ourselves away in isolation has always been an essential part of our craft. Yet it is also often the most challenging factor. We struggle to find space for creativity amidst our hectic professional and social lives. Suddenly, between furloughs, cancelled plans and stay at home orders, it seemed one silver lining might be – 'Finally, I'll have time to write!'

But one thing we discovered is that writing can start to feel all too raw when you are living through a turbulent, transformative moment in history. When so much is happening and there's so much worth writing about, just living through it in the first place, and making sense of those experiences, is not a process that easily inspires pen to paper. The events which have connected us globally in such a short span took time to sink in as we found ourselves facing a future even less secure than we had previously imagined. Yet, through giving ourselves and our little press that time and space to breathe, new stories in fragile forms and sharp shapes came flooding to our inbox. New voices were born, and those that were shaken by the ongoing crisis came back stronger, and with even more to say.

As with our previous collection, Odd Voices, our ten finalists hail from all over the globe, telling the stories of progressive youth from all walks of life. To set the tone for these characters and the challenges they face, we decided to turn not to a fellow author, but to an innovative educator to provide our foreword. Scott Lankford PhD is an English professor at Foothill College, California, who teaches specialist courses in both Climate Change Writing and British Children's Literature. As someone who works with emerging young writers and activists, we knew he could paint us a vivid picture of our teens of tomorrow and the many troubling issues that they find laid at their feet.

FOREWORD

By Professor Scott Lankford

As someone who grew up in the 60s and 70s, I remember the idealism of the baby boomers only too well. We were the first to think we could stop wars and stand up for civil rights. The first to learn of the earth's warming climate. We always said we would be the generation to change the world. And we did. Forever. Irrecoverably. Alas.

We were aware and we were not aware. We were fed lies and told not to worry about our futures by rich companies sowing doubt to secure their profits. Fast forward fifty years, and these days too many older people have abandoned the responsibility of adulthood. The children have become the adults now. The Greta Thunbergs of the world are having to say, 'Go on and sit there. The rest of us need to do something'. They have no choice. They are the ones who realize there's no Planet B. No lifeboats to abandon ship. We're steaming towards so many icebergs and if they hit us, then we'll all go down together.

As an English Professor at Foothill College in California, I have been the founder of our campus's Hypo-Centre for a

Sustainable Future. I also teach a specialist course in Climate Change Education. My class is made up of a delightful and delicious rainbow of students – a group that is international and intersectional, minority majority in its racial demographic, and with many who identify as queer and gender non-conforming. The ages of my students range from 16-year-olds to 86-year-olds, and across this diverse spectrum, the big commonality that brings us together is a passion for our planet and its future.

During the last few years, world events have challenged us more than ever before. My students have been out in the streets, getting tear gassed at peaceful protests. They have lived through the worst droughts and the most apocalyptic wildfires recorded in the history of our state. Now with the pandemic, they have been losing their relatives, or their family's income, due to the Covid crisis. The young people living through these times are being confronted with truths that were always there. Truths their elders knew were there. Only it's inescapable now. It's life threatening, life altering, and they're seeing it the same way we saw a knee on George Floyd's neck for nine and a half minutes. It was a teenage girl who filmed that with her new technology. And that's where my hope lies right now. In this new generation with the desire in their hearts and the power in their hands to change things.

I don't like to call them Generation Z. It's much too grim. I prefer to say Generation A because I feel like they represent the beginning of something, not the end. They are growing up at the time of the Anthropocene and our civilization is coming of age with them. What the hell is going on and where do we go from here? They have to think differently to deal with the altering world around them and this change in mindset is going to be extremely decisive for the future of our planet. With movements like 'Me Too', 'Black Lives Matter' and 'Fridays for Future', there has been a very progressive shift in consciousness. In the US we had 'March for our Lives' and I think a lot of people my age thought 'Thank God! Young people are finally standing up and taking on the NRA!' But then so much of that energy was crushed by the gun lobby and by the cynicism of our polarized electorate.

But I still have hope. The truth isn't something that we can hide from any longer. It is time for a new world. But what form will it take? It is said that authors write the first draft of history. That their stories project possible futures. Not just technological advancements, but our psychological evolution too. You have to look to novelists and poets and artists to try to navigate what's happening. YA fiction in particular has to speak to the politically aware and active youth population we have right now. It has to get behind their movements and hope they will change the way our society thinks forever. Times are changing and this is the generation that wilfully understands the crisis point is upon us.

A Professor of English at Foothill College in Silicon Valley, **Scott Lankford** completed his PhD in Modern Thought and Literature at nearby Stanford University in 1991 with a dissertation on eco-history. In 2010, his book Tahoe Beneath the Surface was awarded a Bronze Medal for Nature Book of the Year by Foreword Magazine. He currently serves as Director of Communication for the Stanford Global Educator's Network and YouTube GEN Channel, where he has helped lead a climate-change-across-the-curriculum initiative for college educators.

The Brief Death Of Aparna

Shreyas Muthusankar

"Present!"

Ram Shankar raised a limp hand for roll call, curious as to why his classmates were so grave and distressed this hot morning. In every direction, the long faces of his classmates were lined and pallid. They sat hunched at their desks, backs arched and heads hanging heavy. Despite much contemplation, his classmates' tears provided no answer, and their balled fists held no explanation inside them.

Ms. Rupa's chin remained high and her gaze wooden behind her gold-frame glasses. She was not the least inclined to inquire after the class' anxieties. Roll call progressed uninterrupted, and the day continued to be bright and sweaty and nervous.

For three periods, discipline quelled curiosity as Ram focused on his studies.

As the world began to swelter in earnest, the students were excused for breakfast.

Breakfast time often began with an eruption of clamour, conversation, and gossip. That day, depressed murmurs trickled inwards from the far corners of the room. Students huddled together, searching for hands that needed holding, though there were fewer shoulders to dry their tears.

Most of Ram's few friends had gone to commiserate with others over this phantom distress, leaving him wanting for company. Luckily, Ved was sitting alone.

Ved cut a thinner silhouette next to Ram's more rounded figure, and he had more eyes behind his head than the average teenager. They had similar intellect, similar grades, and wore similar sacred strings around their torsos. The only Brahmins in their class, the two boys were drawn together by their shared denunciation of meat and their distinct, Sanskrit-stained Tamil.

"Why's everyone...well, like that? Gloomy?" Ram gestured to the class.

Ved's lips were thin. Sweat dripped into his collar. "Aparna's dead."

Ram's eyes went blank. "Huh?"

"She was killed, apparently," Ved said, nursing a spectral pain in his temples.

Ram's eyes whipped to the back of the class. Aparna's seat was empty. "What do you mean she was killed? How?"

"I don't know. They're all so emotional that I can't find a good opportunity to ask them."

As his thoughts ran rampant, Ram's mind went back to that morning. "We could ask Ms. Rupa. She seemed like she knew something."

After a moment in consideration, Ved nodded. They navigated their way to the Teachers' Office.

They soon arrived outside a chamber half-filled with men of meagre repute and great girth, sitting on high-rise chairs with their breakfast open on the table and their shirts unbuttoned partway. The other half was composed of respected women of varying ages, most with heavy gold *thirumangalya* tied around their necks, sacred chains of matrimony. They were seated similarly, though unlike their male counterparts, wore thick, layered sarees that threatened heatstroke even to those who gazed at them.

One stood next to the water purifier to get a drink. Two chatted by the window, indulging in the friendly breeze. Some were on their phones, squinting from behind their spectacles. But all of them turned around to look at the two students who had arrived unceremoniously at the door.

Excusing themselves to go inside, and drawing glares from the discomforted teachers, Ram and Ved stood beside the presently preoccupied Ms. Rupa.

It is still unknown what manner of genuflection the student must extend to their teacher in order to garner attention and affection, but Ram and Ved certainly did not have the answer. She did not meet her eyes with Ram's, nor did she acknowledge their presence through word or gesture.

They waited for her to finish her breakfast while standing uncomfortably in the middle of a room filled with people capable of punishing them on a whim, though they hoped none would aspire to do so. The incongruence between their positions in society versus their role in an educational institution produced a fleeting, yet perpetual dissonance.

Inside that room, Ram and Ved were two inferiors, but the existence of a world outside, where they were the holders of power, was a reality to which the residents of the room, though resistant, were not ignorant.

18

"What do you want?" Ms. Rupa finally asked, wiping her mouth.

"Ms. Rupa, we wanted to know what happened to Aparna, if you're fine with telling us?" Ram tried his best not to offend her, for she took umbrage to the most common of things.

But Ms. Rupa scoffed at once. "Her? The little wench tried to run away from home with some *parayan*. What else did she expect?"

Ram and Ved frowned violently.

"She was killed because she was in love with a Dalit?" Ved asked, giving voice to his thoughts, perhaps with the intention of declaring the irrationality of the statement. However, all he received in return was a nod of reassurance that she had deserved it.

No killer was named by Ms. Rupa, but it was unnecessary.

Dalit. *Parayan*. Outcaste.

It would not do for the daughter to make decisions on her own about matters that directly affected the honour of their family, least of all one as important as marriage. It was not her place. The gravity of repercussions for threatening the dignity of her blood was only natural. The iron hammer must fall, and the father's hand must hold it.

"I'll tell you what her problem was," Ms. Rupa continued unprompted, "She had no self-discipline, just like the rest of you teenagers. None of you have self-discipline. If you did, you wouldn't give up to your lust and make all these brash decisions. Falling in love with the first boy you see, it's just lust."

She seemed to find no qualms with punishing a girl with death for lack of discipline, nor with preaching vehemently to two boys who only wished to inquire after the murder of their classmate.

"Don't make the same mistakes as her." She paused before glancing at Ved. "Although, I'm sure *some of you* will be forgiven."

Ved's eyes narrowed, though he turned his eyes away before Ms. Rupa noticed. It was common knowledge that Ved's father had married someone below his stature, but it was mostly forgiven—with the understanding that it would be criticised heavily and frequently. His wife's family were wealthy and held a respectable position, so her lower blood was compensated with a fulsome dowry.

Ved did not respond to Ms. Rupa's jibe. "Thank you, ma'am." He nodded and turned around to leave. Ram responded with a belated echo of "Thank you, ma'am," and followed behind him.

For the rest of that day, Ved proceeded to crease or tear every page of a book he turned, and his handwriting grew thick, dark, and angular. Ram forced himself to refocus on his studies and took notes religiously.

The sun's noontime blaze began to grow tame as the clock's hands closed to 3:30PM. Class was over, and everyone prepared for their commute back home. The gardener was committed to his lawn mower, running it over beds of greenery bordering the pavement. The scent of mutilated grass diffused through the air on the way to the school gates, momentarily subduing the confusion that gripped the minds of any who knew that the population of the school had been permanently reduced by one.

As the evening breeze made the Earth calmer and more reasonable, Ram left Ved to his own devices, as he often did when he seemed disturbed.

Once again left wanting for company, he sought out Syed, who was gathered with a group of agitated teenagers. Most of their names he could not readily recall, but he knew the three leading them.

Raja, Syed and Fathima were his classmates, and were most often seen together with Aparna. While they were quite popular on their own, the absence of that single number seemed jarring enough to be unnatural. Ram overheard their discussions, and gleaned that they had planned to visit Aparna's home and confirm what had happened.

Unlike Ram, these were people who had met and known Aparna's father for themselves. They could not come to terms with the fact that he had allowed it.

Just as Syed spotted Ram standing behind him, he walked over to them with a feigned shrug. "What are you guys doing?"

Raja and Syed looked at Ram calling after them, initially hesitant, but soon they beckoned to him. As he approached their group, he felt that he must seem terribly out of place amidst their concentration of despondent frustration.

"We're going to visit Aparna's house. We need to find out if the rumours are true or not." Syed spoke with a low and venomous voice.

In almost every memory that Ram had of Syed, he remembered one of the other three around him. They had known each other from the time they began school. Raja and Fathima would get into trouble for trying to skip class, or organising a cake party during class hours, or for drawing graffiti on the school compound wall, and Syed and Aparna, being student council members, would bear the burden of getting them out of trouble. Despite multiple excoriations, Raja and Fathima remained faithful to their chaotic tendencies, and Aparna and Syed remained close friends with them, in spite of their temperamental differences.

In contrast here was Ram: an awkward novelty of a Tamil boy, who did not discriminate so much as make himself incapable of fitting in with crowds which he did not like. He had nothing to do with their group besides being acquainted with one of them.

Just as he was about to leave and return them to their earlier purity of conviction, he spied the silhouette of Ved approaching from the corner of his vision.

The serenity of grassy fields was lost, and instead the smoke of motor vehicles and the sporadic blare of vehicle horns framed their senses. In the midst of this was a boy who had clearly listened in on their plan, and appropriated it for himself.

"I'm coming with you," Ved declared. Consequently, Ram was forced to participate against the wishes of too many.

A good half hour later, a decision was made. There were ten students in their party, with Raja, Syed, and Fathima making up the vanguard. Their backs were the straightest, though Ram feared they were similarly the most prone to breaking.

Ram and Ved did not contribute a single word on the way there, each preoccupied with his own thoughts. Ram's were a preoccupation of what Ved's thoughts might have been.

As someone whose parents experienced the villainy of prejudice to this day, where every misfortune was blamed on a single decision and every rational defence was met with backlash of the most primitive, indefensible kind, Ved's investment in the issue could not be little.

After the third share-auto trip, they got off and regrouped together outside Thevar Bazaar for the last leg of the journey.

Thevar Bazaar was a bustling shopping market for all manner of commodities, from watches to flat-screen televisions. There were bicycle shops and shops to repair the bicycles. There were butchers and restaurants to buy the butchered fowl. It was a place where quality was left to chance, frequented by middle-aged wives and resourceful teenagers keen on fulfilling their fiscal responsibilities, which had in their cases become a necessity.

Thevar Bazaar had dozens of shops in two rows on either side of the narrow road, with no place to disembark from one's vehicle without greatly irritating the overspill of road-goers that perpetually populated the bazaar. The bazaar began as abruptly as it ended, forever covered by a translucent layer of dust and noise and rage.

It was a ten-minute walk to Aparna's home, and the bazaar's trinkets attracted Ram's attention away from the gravity of their endeavour. He let his eyes wander from shop to shop, examining each display briefly before moving on to the next unruly stack of objects.

For a moment more, he observed the small ring-necked parakeet chick in one of the long cages suspended from the ceiling of *Rasappa Parrat Shop*. It was a miniscule thing with barely enough feathers to cover its body, small enough that it could squeeze through the bars and escape if it were careless. Unaware of such a privilege, it remained nested within its cage.

A shortcut through a very narrow alley—though apparently not so narrow that two motorcyclists did not think it imprudent to try and cross each other—led them to a stunted street with four houses in a row.

House 9/31 was Aparna's home, occupied now by some small garlands, a mother and father, an uncle on the father's side, and a body in an ice box delivered to them by the police.

Bharat and Jyoti sat on the mosaic floor of their home with tears held back in their eyes, staring with melancholy admonishment into the transparent box.

Syed and Raja barged in before taking a sharp breath. They were a step too late, and Fathima caught sight of the truth, where before it was merely words amidst a rumour.

Aparna's greying body was in a forest-green saree, dressed impeccably by Jyoti. The fatal injury was hidden beneath layers of silk and self-righteousness.

Fathima wailed suddenly, calling out Aparna's name again and again, and battering the ice box with weak, loud ferocity. Raja and Syed forced their hearts to stay in place, working instead to pacify her. The others, whom Ram did not know, were transfixed by the image.

They took no note of the tears streaming down Bharat's face.

He would have to live with the shame that his daughter had chosen some other boy over her own blood, that he was a poor husband and father. He would live with that indignity for all his life.

That evening, as the sun dipped down into the ground, everyone's friendly Bharat uncle took a stand as tears and screams of anguish clawed into his skin.

"I understand that you're all sad about what happened. I merely ask that you be mature about this, and consider it from an objective point of view before condemning us." Bharat seemed fully prepared to explain himself. Ram looked at Bharat's wrinkles and his soft, bleary pupils, but could not readily find a murderer in them.

The greater a person's age, the more acutely aware they became of how emotional and ambivalent the teenage creature was, and how inconsiderate it was of an adult's considerations. Indeed, Bharat must have been a soft man, Ram thought, as he chose to address their group despite that fact. Bharat knew almost every one of those gathered, and they knew him in return. He must have supposed that they would understand

"Aparna…was found to be having illicit affairs with a boy from a different community. When we found out, we obviously tried to reason with her. We told her that she couldn't be with someone of a lower caste." Bharat spat out some of those words. Jyoti remained sobbing on the ground.

Syed came forward. "Uncle, are you responsible for this?"

The older man's eyes twitched as he drew in a sharp breath. Steadily, he spoke again. "There were several parties involved. My pleas were rendered useless, and many were... of the impression that it was our duty to maintain the purity of our blood."

Disbelief shattered any hopes the children might have had that this was a separate incident. Perhaps that she had been killed by some street mugger or a serial killer, for that must have been a kinder fate for everyone.

Ved's eyes were wide, still seized by the daughter's body in the ice box.

Ram had never seen Bharat in the flesh before, but he had the impression that this person was significantly older today than he had been a handful of days ago. He seemed to be struggling with himself, at the decisions he had made, as though his blood were running backwards. Ram's veins emerged along his temples, but looking at Bharat's trembling fingers, at his eyes that only wanted to close, he found a hint of pity.

"I want you to listen to me. The boy she wanted to be with was called Ashok. He was a resourceful boy, and as far as I could tell, he genuinely liked Aparna. Of course, you're all teenagers, so there's no need to speak about love and such things, but just being seen in public with the boy would shatter her prospect of a happy marriage in the future."

Raja was about to interject, but he was stopped by a raised hand from Bharat. "The boy's father was a construction worker, and his mother had a lame leg. Aparna would have had no future whatsoever. Beyond all else, my ultimate motive is to give her a happy life. If she had given up on the boy, then no matter what our relatives said about her, we could take care of it. I would fight anyone for my daughter, you know that," he said, and indeed they did. "However..." His palm folded into a fist as it rose up.

His expression twisted.

Rage. Disappointment. Betrayal. Colourful emotions spread across his face.

"She ran away! Left the home she grew up in, her father, her mother! All to be with that bastard Dalit!"

His closed fist smashed down onto the ice box.

Aparna's body fell askew in its frigid chamber. Jyoti jumped with a cry, gluing herself to the box and pleading heavily to her husband to forgive their daughter, at least in death.

It was at that moment that Raja, Syed, Fathima and the group came to a terrible realisation. Just as much as they were outraged at Aparna's murder, Bharat was just as outraged at being put in a position of participating in it.

Perhaps, even more so.

The evening sun sunk into the earth in its entirety. The last rays of light entering through the window faded away.

The dusk of Aparna's death had arrived.

Under the sinking light, enlightenment flooded in like a shattered dam.

They were ten small, meaningless children, nothing more. Raja, a boy with voluminous hair and pale, brown skin. Fathima, her *pardah* fallen partially over her head, unable to bear the intensity of her sorrow. Syed, with barely enough facial hair to form a beard, despite seventeen years of waiting.

Ved, an invisible abomination within his own society.

17-year-old adolescents of the human species. Some with blacker skin than brown. Some with pale, reddish flesh. Some wearing *pardahs,* some wearing *poonals.* None of them were the same anymore.

Lines of symmetry rose between every pair of people in the room. Though these lines reflected that they were all related in some sincere, irredeemable way, the divisions placed each of them, to different extents, on opposing sides.

There was no longer any singular similarity among them that could overcome the differences which had emerged around the girl in the ice box.

Fathima recovered slowly, standing up and readjusting her fallen *pardah.*

For a moment, she opened her mouth as if to speak, but Fathima closed it when she, like Ram, noticed the presence of a third party in the house.

This was a fat man, sitting on the chair with one leg over his thighs, listening with languid attention to the scene as though he was watching the final moments of a play.

He was a faceless individual: an amalgamation of centuries of depravity and perversion. His children's identities would be effaced, just as his was. Kind, gentle people would be born whose every contribution would be attributed to some faceless, distorted, viciously unpardonable concept, an existence that cannot be reasoned with, for indeed, a concept merely exists, dead and unmoving. It exerts influence on all things with force and odium. It made their words either black or white, with no clear distinction as to which was the righteous and which the immoral, merely that they were pure and absolute opposites that may not be resolved without mutual destruction.

This faceless, fat concept observed with impunity, imperial in its grotesqueness. There was no arguing with a concept, and Fathima was the first to recognise it.

Ram jumped when she liberated from her tongue mere vitriol. "You killed your daughter. You killed an innocent child. You're a murderer and a fraud. There is no salvation for you. Not in life, nor in death."

The others did very little to contain their emotions, save for expressing it through violence. Ved remained quieter than the corpse. Bharat stood stalwart, hiding a frail Jyoti behind him, both already crippled by the prologue to their future playing out in front of them.

Inevitably, the group turned their backs on house 9/31 and walked themselves out into a more violent world, suddenly more shackled, more restricted and insane.

Ved and Ram followed behind the others, the former's jaw clenched closed.

"How are you feeling?"

Ved took a deep breath. "Oh, I don't know."

The noise of Thevar Bazaar grew closer and closer with each step.

"I don't know if I should feel lucky that I was born, or sad that others won't get to make the same decision about their children, or happy again that they won't have to go through the utter agony that my parents have gone through." He turned to Ram. "What about you?"

Ram sighed. "I don't know. I'll probably think clearer in a while. I'm just wondering if my parents care that much about caste too. Like, would they drive me out if I said I liked a non-Brahmin someday?"

"Your parents don't care about caste." Ved's nails dug into his palm. "If they did, you would know that Raja is a Chettiar, and Aparna was a Mukkulathoor Thevar, and you would *care* that Syed is a Muslim. You would care about those things, because they're significant to you as a person, and they exist in direct opposition to you and everything you were birthed to stand for."

The day turned colder with every passing moment, seeping through the dust and smoke of Thevar Bazaar.

Ved shook his head at Ram. "I bet you don't even know where a Chettiar and a Thevar stand in the hierarchy. As far as Indian kids go, you're about as privileged as can be. If I married someone, and she wasn't a proper Iyer Brahmin, how much would you bet that my grandparents would drive me out of my home and take away my inheritance?"

Ram's eyes were stuck to the ground. "It shouldn't be a privilege to love a woman. I'm not privileged, everyone else is crippled."

Ved clenched his teeth. "Sure."

Ram noticed that the group was not heading back on the same route. Despite noticing the unplanned detour, they stayed silent.

Ram chose to dwell on Aparna further. "Still, isn't it strange that Aparna had a boyfriend at all?"

"How do you mean?" Ved asked, keeping a wary eye on the road.

"It's like you said. She would have known about his caste and stuff, right? And if she knew her parents were going to object to such a degree, then why go through with it at all? I didn't know her all that well, but she had a safety-first approach, right?"

Ved stared at him. "She was in love, Ram. I doubt she was being very rational."

"No, actually." Syed piped in from somewhere ahead.

It transpired that everyone was listening in on their conversation. Ram slowed down his pace and rubbed the back of his neck. "Um, how do you mean?"

Syed slowed to match his pace. "She was very rational. She knew what was possible for her and what wasn't. She knew exactly what her parents would do if she said she liked a man from a different caste." The boy grunted. "I'm talking like she wanted to marry Ashok. No, that wasn't even on the table. They liked each other a lot and supported each other emotionally. She wanted to be an engineer and earn a ton of money, that's what she really wanted to do. Bridal clothes were not a part of her vision for the future.

"Anyways, the point is, everyone knew that Bharat Uncle was too soft to ever willingly hurt his own daughter." Ram and Ved had gleaned such an impression from him, at least initially.

The group turned into a narrow alley cut up with clotheslines, right outside *Rasappa Parrat Shop*. It was dimly lit, with an electricity pole standing in the middle of it.

"It wasn't Bharat Uncle." Raja interjected. "He killed his daughter, that's for sure, but it wasn't him. Aparna's uncle, Gambir. He arrived in town less than a week ago. He's the one who discovered Ashok. He was in the house too, remember?" Ram nodded, remembering the silent fat man. Fathima shuddered in front of them. "We all knew that Aparna's father would have forgiven her if she wanted to pursue a relationship with Ashok, but Gambir found out before him. He festered this illusion that his daughter had gone on the wrong path, and he needed to be harsher, even though she would never have done anything without asking him in the first place. Gambir made life hell for Aparna in the five days he was with them, and she had no choice but to run away. Bharat uncle lost trust in Aparna because Gambir *made* him lose trust in his daughter."

Ram suddenly realised that the group was no longer alone. In the dead centre of the alley was a boy standing under an electricity pole. His dark brown skin glistened with sweat and burned him where it ran over his horribly scraped leg. His eyes jittered, like he had too much to say. Ram could guess who the boy must have been.

"And?" Ashok said.

Slowly, Syed pulled out his phone to show the boy a picture. "Bharat Uncle...was involved."

Aparna's corpse was just as motionless and subdued in the picture as she was in reality.

Ashok screamed, clutching the phone in his hand. His knees plummeted to the floor.

The others crowded around him, pulling him back up and pacifying him as best they could.

Raja, a beat slower, stood back and watched, clenching his fist to contain its trembling.

Ram approached him with quiet steps. "Raja, what happened that day, exactly?"

Ashok's eyes pooled with ugly tears, as if all he could see was that haunting afternoon flashing through his eyes, over and over.

Raja took a moment, his lips quivering as he began the tale. "Aparna ran away from home after seeing how her father started to treat her after Gambir arrived."

Ram could imagine it himself. That quiet, cloudy afternoon with dragonflies buzzing around him.

"They were being pursued by some of Gambir's men. Friends, relatives, who knows."

Ashok running from those old, rugged men with *aruvals* in their hands, who knew less of harvesting crop than murdering children.

"He was barely able to hide himself, but Aparna was caught before she could get away."

Ram could picture that small bit of afternoon, barely seen through the gap in the cargo crate, and the puddle of blood, and the body that lay in it.

Raja inhaled sharply. "Fuck those casteist bastards."

"I shouldn't have asked her to stay with me," Ashok cried out. His voice was hoarse and broken. "She could have stayed with Fathima. She would have been fine. But I said I'd keep her safe…" He choked up, biting hard into his lips.

"Listen, I know you guys were being nice and all, but Ashok is in a bad way right now, so…" Raja trailed off, but his intentions were clear.

And so, with a curt nod and quick goodbyes, Ved and Ram left without ceremony or resolution.

When they re-entered Thevar Bazaar, *Rasappa Parrat Shop* was feeding its finches and its parakeets.

Selling ring-necked parrots was illegal in India, but it was typically overlooked, especially in a space like Thevar Bazaar, where shops change every two years.

The ring-neck's cage was open. A caretaker was carefully refilling its food, massaging the parrot's neck with a smile. The parrot let out a comfortable noise, clearly cosy in his hands.

Ram sighed. "Like a mirror."

"Huh?" Ved asked, snapped out of his stupor.

Ram shook his head. "Nothing." They proceeded onwards, retracing their steps through Thevar Bazaar.

They waited to cross the road to the other side. At the next opening, they trudged through the traffic.

"What are you thinking?" Ved asked.

Ram contemplated the question. "I don't think anything will change because of this. Her family will go through hell, and I have next to no pity for them. Every community has people like Gambir in them, including ours, and they ruin everything. The fact that Bharat succumbed to their demands makes it all the more aggravating."

They arrived at the entrance of the Bazaar and hailed an auto-rickshaw.

Ram shook his head. "I don't have anything to say about it. It's always been like this, and it will continue to be. The same with

Aparna and Ashok. It's fine to love, but they also needed to prepare for the worst. To be prudent about it." The stuttering engine roared to life, coughing out pits of black smoke. Thevar Bazaar began to move farther and farther away.

"You're sounding more and more like Ms. Rupa."

Ram raised a brow at the comparison, and quickly hoped to redeem himself. "Of course, the fault of the murder still lies with the family, and I'm not so base as to go to a funeral and speak ill of the dead. What happened with Aparna was horrible and unfortunate, but that's how it is, and I'm afraid that's how it always will be in the world."

"Aparna." The auto driver piped up. He had a large beard and smelled like he hadn't had a sip of beer his entire life. "Bharat's daughter? You're from Meenakshi Higher Sec, right?"

Ram responded with a stutter. "Uh, yes."

The driver turned his attention back to the road. "We'll all die."

"Excuse me?"

"Us old people. Give it a few decades, and we'll die like dominos, one after another. You're right to say that it's always been like this, but it doesn't need to be in the future. Be patient."

Ram and Ved stayed silent for the rest of the trip. The auto-rickshaw stuttered forwards reliably, letting them off at their respective stops. They went home, had measly dinners and went to bed.

Information about Aparna's death had spread rapidly through the school by the next morning. More people came to know about the crime, and a killer was apprehended. There was media coverage, but it quickly died down, as there were always more crimes to cover, and greater moral quandaries to tarnish with politics. Talk happened on every street corner as Ram made his way to class.

"Is it a crime to love someone?" He heard a middle-aged lady say to her friend.

"You can sugar-coat it all you want. The fact is, the girl ran away with someone she shouldn't be with. What did she expect? India is like that, after all." The other lady replied.

"But did she deserve to be killed?"

"The media spoke about it. No one cared. It didn't even become national news. We're just a small city, not Chennai or Delhi. Nobody cares what happens here. Besides, the girl wasn't even that young. She was 17! The media wants sensation. Something like: '12-year-old Muslim girl in Kashmir raped by Hindu temple priest, caught on camera,' and all that."

"It's almost laughable how a woman trying to be with someone she loves gets the same punishment as a man raping and murdering a small child."

"Almost."

Ram never saw their faces, but the road diverged, and he sprinted west to school. Passing through the gates, he rushed into class without a moment to spare.

Aparna's seat remained vacant, and he assumed it would remain vacant the entire year.

Aparna's death was a brief event for the world. Certainly, it did not survive for very long in the minds of news-watchers. But the students of Meenakshi Sec. would, most likely, carry the incident with them their entire lives.

Ram sat down at his bench with Ved beside him.

Ms. Rupa entered the classroom before Ved could speak, and demanded a moment of silence. "Just as you have responsibilities towards your teachers, you have responsibilities towards your parents for the freedom they give you. You need to consider their needs as your first priority. That's the absolute least amount of respect you need to show them, if you love your parents." Her *thirumangalyam* gleamed against the sun.

"Listen here. Your parents pay good money to let you study in a school with good facilities and teachers. They're giving you freedom. Do not abuse it. Did you hear me? Do not-" She paused there.

"Abuse it." The class responded in chorus.

Fathima, Syed and Raja had their eyes glued to their desks. Ram mouthed the words, though no sound was produced.

Ved remained quiet. He shook his head only once.

"What?" Ram asked quietly.

"I can't fathom the depth of the bullshit that just came out of her mouth."

Ms. Rupa glared at Ved, recognising a challenge to her authority. "Stand outside, Ved."

"Freedom, she says." He smiled derisively, walking outside.

Class began once more, and Ram focused once again on his studies.

Peace had been restored.

.

Shreyas Muthusankar is a Second Year International Student at the University of Birmingham pursuing an Undergraduate in English and Creative Writing. His hometown is Madurai, Tamil Nadu, and his Indian heritage is something he has explored and contemplated since childhood. He spends most of his time watching Anime or reading books. He is in the extremely privileged position of having been born in a family that supports his truant wishes, and justifies his passion for writing with his overconfidence and his unfounded hopes of a successful career.

Maasai Lights

Mary Ball Howkins

Sironka (*the clean one, pure* in Maa)
Legishon (*the polite one* in Maa)

I hate lions. Lions ate my family's only bull so we can no longer bring new calves into the Savannah to feed our community or increase our wealth. Here in the Nairobi National Park, we have been killing the lions who steal our cattle, goats and sheep. Killing a lion is forbidden by the government, but it can still bring great power and status to a Maasai warrior. There are not many lions left in the park and our government wants us to live in peace with them. But how can you live in peace with a lion who eats cows? It's not possible unless you learn to understand them. To understand them, you must see how they behave.

My grandmother asked me to find a solution to lions feasting on our animals.

"Sironka, the lions have killed another calf. You must stand watch in the night to stir up some trouble for them." She leaned out of our doorway steadying her frail body by the pole in the weave of the wall.

"It's not safe to stand guard over the animals in the cow shed at night. I could become a tasty lion meal." I turned toward her, shaking my head. "Not my fate, I hope."

I smiled faintly. Grandmother nodded her head. It is bald like the heads of many grandmothers, so it shines in the afternoon sun.

"I know that, but you must try something," she said. "We are losing too many cows and sheep. Of course I want you to be safe. Think of something that will frighten the lions while you sleep."

The next morning, I woke up with an idea. Animals are afraid of fire, so I set about gathering some dead branches to build a fire in our kraal. I didn't have to go far to find enough wood. Elephants had torn down branches in their travels and other trees had died of old age, shedding plenty of dry wood for a big fire.

"Legishon, help me drag wood back into the center of the kraal."

He glowered, then tilted his head up like a question.

My brother, Legishon, was eleven, and strong, perhaps stronger than me if I am honest. I was thirteen and had herded our animals longer than he. Some Maasai boys who have only learned to walk begin to take charge of a family's cows. I took charge at age nine.

"I will if you stop taking our radio apart. I want to listen to music. You are not a real Maasai boy. You would rather take Mamma's radio apart and rebuild it than build warrior strength." Every day he chided me about what a poor warrior I made.

The first time I took her radio my mother chased me out of the house screaming. Her radio sat on a small shelf. She wanted to reach me with a walking stick to beat me, but when she saw that I could put the radio back together again she forgave me. If I could find old radios in town to trade for Maasai beads, I could build radios with better reception.

The wood pile reached high and wide. "That's enough wood," I said, fully confident that my experiment would work.

"Legishon, you get the dung. Make sure it's dry. I will get the fire-maker and some dry grasses."

"It's not easy to make a fire last all night," he said with his elbows jutting from his sides and a scowl on his narrow face. He looked at the wood we had gathered; he was right. Our fires are short ones, mostly for cooking.

"We will start a small fire and then pile on the big branches later to make it last."

We are both good with the fire-maker. Maasai don't use matches. We use a thick wooden slab with a round hole and a round stick to rotate in it. It takes a lot of practice, as well as patience, to know when to blow on the grasses and dry cow dung to get flames started.

We Maasai believe we came from heaven with our cows and land at the beginning of time. Our cows and the land are precious to us and make us strong. When given in friendship, cows bind together our large family communities. Lions threaten the sacred gifts that bind us all.

When I piled on the biggest branches, Legishon was full of worry. He threw his hands in the air, jumped and yelled: "You are going to burn down our whole boma, Sironka. Our family's security circle is made of thorny acacia, dry and ready to catch fire."

"No, I'm not going to burn it all down. We need this fire to last long into the night. These logs will collapse on themselves as they burn. Besides, ours is a large kraal with wide open areas for the animals."

"What about the embers?" he whined. "They can fly to our house."

"I will wait to see how high the fire climbs and then sleep with one eye open. We can put a bucket of water at the edge of the fire just in case."

That night was long, sleeping with one eye open sometimes, and sometimes not. Lions came all the same. Before sleeping we saw that the light from the fire made the inside of the cow shed even more visible than before. They could see their meal and must have simply walked around the fire into the shed. A cow's bloody carcass lay near the entrance to our boma. A lion had eaten the animal as usual from its backside, pulling the hind legs out of its way in a bloody mess. My idea had failed. Maybe I was not up to this. My whole body slumped.

"Your idea has cost us another cow," Legishon said from behind in a low mocking voice. "What kind of lion fighter are you, Maasai boy? No warrior like the rest of us."

"I'll show you what a warrior I am," I said and turned to tackle him by the ankles and pinned him by his arms. Fortunately,

Grandmamma peered out of the door or he probably would have dumped me on my back.

"Thank you for trying," Grandmamma said as she walked toward the burnt pile. "Burn the carcass before the jackals come around, and don't give up. Both of you use the embers to get the fire going again. She kicked a bit of left-over wood, lifting some ash and embers under her long, sand-colored skirt without harm. "When it's done, I will sweep earth over the fire spot to make it new again."

Two days later I kicked at the ground where the fire had been. I turned toward my sneering brother. "Legishon, let's try something else."

He looked at me with weary eyes, then down at his feet. "What now, Sironka? More useless ideas?" His long face seemed even longer as he backed away as if getting ready to get out of earshot or dive behind our hut.

He has always thought that all of my ideas would drag him into something he really didn't want to be involved in.

"A scarecrow," I shouted. "I've seen them in gardens to keep away birds, monkeys and small animals. Maybe a scarecrow would fool a lion. I could dress it to look like me, tall and dark, with my most ragged white-people's clothes,"

Legishon turned back and perked up: "I suppose a pretend man might keep a lion away, maybe if you made it soft so the arms could move in a breeze. The more alive it could look, the better it might work. We could stuff the clothes with straw to give them form and make it look like you, brother. Any lion would run away fast."

That smirk I often see on his face was there again.

"Come on," I urged, ignoring his tease and straightening up tall, "Help look for an old shirt and trousers, not any precious Maasai clothing, and lots of straw. I'll get one of our straight building poles already stripped and waiting to be driven into the ground."

He seemed game, maybe only to harass me. I hoped this idea would work, but some doubt crept into my mind.

Together we pounded the pole in front of the cowshed, keeping our eyes on the calves at the same time, to make sure they didn't bolt from the noise. Then we assembled a fellow we called Leboo, which means 'born in the bush'. We called him that since his insides were dry bush grass. He was handsome. His arms had little straw where they met the shoulders, so they swung loose and could move when a breeze came. Legishon liked Leboo so much he forgot he wanted to make him look like me.

In the morning he and I arrived at the shed the same moment when light first made it visible.

I was amazed. "Look. Not one cow is missing."

"Success!" we shouted together, jumping up and down and scaring the calves, so that they hid behind their mothers. "No lions!"

We told everyone we saw that the new way to fool lions was to make a scarecrow with soft arms that moved. Legishon was almost as proud as I was. The news traveled, and Maasai from close by visited to see how we did it. Really, though, the lions fooled us. The next morning, we learned that the lions were smarter than we thought. They had already figured out Leboo was a fake and had just walked around him to make another kill. The whole village went from happiness to disappointment, even despair, overnight. The lions felt no fear and could kill whenever they were hungry again. Another bloody carcass to burn.

"I give up," Legishon said, as he slid down a wall of the shed to look like a bag of potatoes. He was always easily frustrated when it came to anything I did. Did he really want my ideas to succeed? I think not.

"There must be another way," I muttered, but I had no idea what that way might be.

Whatever method we used the next time would have to be tested more than one night, maybe many nights before boasting to so many families. Everyone knew that we had failed. The lions, who followed herds of zebra as they migrated, could raid our cows any time they pleased. Our cows are so precious to us. They give us the milk and blood to drink and live well.

Days passed with the two of us in school, uniforms paid for by the crops we sell, but we found no solution to the lion problem. Then one night I was walking outside our boma with a flashlight and felt a presence close to me. If I ran, a predator would view me as more of a prey, so I waited then turned my body slightly in slow motion. I let my flashlight search in a quick sweep of the direction I felt the presence. The light caught the face of a female lion, and after seconds, a snapping sound trailed into the depth of the underbrush. A lion had been close but had run in the other direction, away from me. I stood there for moments thinking about what had just happened. A flashlight in motion; maybe that's what a lion fears. The cats are not just simple predatory creatures.

"Leg-i-shon," I called gasping from back inside our boma. "Lions might be afraid of a moving light."

I doubled over, hands on my knees shaking from excitement. He looked out the door, listening to my panting, but I could see he was doubtful. He had not seen a lion approach and heard it run.

"How do you know?" he asked and walked closer.

I looked up at his face. "One just took off when I walked outside the boma with my flashlight," I said closing my eyes so tightly my head ached.

"You saw it? Was it close?"

I looked up and saw him run his hand over his hair in genuine concern.

"Oh, it was close, alright. I could sense it... only feet away." My breath was still erratic, and it scattered my words. "It was a female, low to the ground, already a stalker. I heard the sounds of it racing away. She was big, maybe hunting for her kits."

I sank to a squat on the ground, breathing hard.

"I am glad you're safe, but you and your ideas, Sironka. Leave this alone. It's not worth getting mutilated or eaten by a lion. That would not be warrior stuff."

"I can't stop... I know there is a way, and I have an idea using the battery in Mamma's radio."

"You're not a real Maasai boy, Sironka. You are too modern with those batteries and your new ideas."

"Yes, I have modern ideas, and if they stop the lions, I will be a strong Maasai boy for having served my community, but not for my physical strength."

I stood up tall to face him and make my point.

"I suppose," Legishon said. His dropping voice sounded like he had little faith in my abilities.

⟫ ⟫ ⟫ ⟫ ⟫

Later Legishon barely noticed as my mother chased me out of our home again, this time with a grass broom in her hands and hoping to give me some whacks on my shoulders or head. I ran as fast as I could with our only good battery, the one from her radio. I flew out of the kraal where I knew she wouldn't follow in case of snakes or predators. I would have to sneak back when she was busy and had forgotten what I had done. For a long time, I waited, seated beneath an acacia tree where I put my lion plan together.

After a few days I brought together all my scavenged electrical bits, along with a small solar panel that I kept from the extras, when panels were installed at my school. The government of Kenya is actively supporting solar energy and hopes to produce half of its electricity soon. We Maasai have the sun here, more than most places in the world, and the technology to bring all Kenyans closer to a better life. We must do it without hesitation.

In the village of our school, where I walked every day, I traded some beads for electrical wire and found two flashlights with broken cases, but with their bulbs still working.

"Legishon. What are you thinking?" He sat at the edge of the kraal opening where I worked hoping that I could escape fast if Mother came after me again. He watched in silence as I attached some of the parts to the kraal poles that protected the cows and us.

Silence.

"Are you trying to live up to your mistaken name, *the polite one*?" I asked. "It's not like you. You're not making fun of my non-warrior-like character. Why? I know, you're probably waiting for another failure."

I ignored his quiet and put together my invention; a solar panel to gather electricity, a battery to store it, a small box I called my transformer. It would send electricity to my two broken flashlights attached to different poles, and a switch to turn on the lights at night and make them blink on and off. The lights faced outward from where the lions often approached. I tested the system, and it worked. The lights blinked. Now I had to wait for night, but I was so excited to find out if the lights worked on the lions that I could barely be still. Legishon was impressed, even though he didn't say so. He examined every part of my invention in a slow, relaxed manner and then gave me a silent pat on the back and walked toward the house. A sort of silent approval? It could be a first.

"It's dusk," I called. "I will set the lights flashing. If there are hungry lions in the area they could come early."

"You just want to admire your work, Sironka. Lions will probably love the lights like the fire and the scarecrow."

He was right about me admiring my own work. No one else in my family was particularly interested in this third experiment because the first two had failed, so I was alone in my excitement. Of course my mother wanted me to give her battery back as soon as the next lion showed up to make a kill. I had to promise that I would return it.

I slept soundly that night and never opened my eyes until my father called my name to say that the cows needed to get out for grazing. I scrambled out the door, having slept in my clothes, and walked to the shed. Legishon was already there grinning at me.

"No kill. But who knows what tomorrow will bring?" he said in a mocking tone.

"You know, Legishon, if this works, I have permission to roll you in cow dung."

"You do not."

"Papa said."

"He would never say that," he answered with his nose in the air, arms crossed.

"I'll do it anyway."

"Just try."

He probably figured that it was an empty threat, and I wasn't sure myself if I meant to go through with it when the time came.

⟫ ⟫ ⟫ ⟫ ⟫

The next morning, and the next and the next, it was obvious that lions not only didn't like moving lights, but that a blinking light might have made them think that a Maasai warrior was walking back and forth standing guard.

"Both you boys know well we Maasai have a special history with lions," Papa began after sitting us down on the short sections of tree stump we used as stools. "They do fear us."

Legishon grinned since he gloried in our Maasai past where lion hunting was a sign of bravery and personal achievement for a hunter on his own.

"Now that lion numbers are down in the park, mostly because of rabies and canine distemper virus," Papa continued, we hunt a lion in a group and preserve the numbers of cats. "We don't hunt females or injured lions, only healthy males. We hunt the traditional way, with a spear and shield, dangerous but fun, and a sign of protecting our land and livestock."

"We know all this Papa," Legishon said with a deep sigh. We were proud of our history with the lion, but Papa had told us the story too many times.

He went on anyway. "When warriors return home with a lion, our celebration lasts for a week, and the first warrior to spear the lion is honored with a special beaded shoulder strap to wear during the celebration. Many Maasai warriors have been lost to lions so when the group returns intact, there is much gratitude and excitement."

We both listened politely.

"We saw the celebration when we were small, almost too small to remember," Legishon said.

"I remember. I was only four, but I remember the joy and pride in our village. I have seen that beaded strap that our village chief guards."

I have repeated my invention for many families whose cows, sheep and goats are precious like ours. Farmers in Kenya are thrilled to have a sound and reliable method to guard their livestock. Lions live among us, along with other predators, yet we respect them and their habits along with our precious cattle. We have coexisted with lions, elephants and other creatures since time began; all of us use the grasslands and woods with equal rights. And we know more about the lions from my first encounter with my flashlight. We can preserve both our family animals and the big cat.

Now it's best to use car batteries and car signal lights that flash instead of the small electrical things that I collected. My lion-fighting invention is known all over Kenya, not just by my people in the south.

I feel so lucky to be a modern Maasai warrior.

As for Legishon, he hasn't yet been rolled in cow dung, but his time will come very soon.

Mary Ball Howkins writes for and about southern African youth. Her stories reveal some of the challenges young Africans face and the successes they achieve against difficult odds, human and animal. Her experiences as an African wildlife, school and orphanage volunteer have informed the narratives she weaves.

Eye Of The Beholder

Alec James

Space is a magnificent sight. Mind-blowingly vast, dazzling to behold. And that's looking up at the night sky from the surface of the Earth. How much more beautiful would it be, if you could see it up close?

Right outside your window.

Teresa Petros, beside a porthole aboard the vast ship Perseus, fought the tears that threatened to push their way into her eyes.

But she wasn't looking at the view.

"You're such a stuck-up bitch, Petros."

"Yeah. Who do you think you are, greaseball?"

"They wouldn't let someone like you be here, if it wasn't for your *dad*."

"Haha. Yeah, good job daddy's rich, huh?"

Teresa didn't waste the energy fighting them. To begin with, she had. She may only have been fourteen, but life had taught her to stand her ground, and usually that brought positive results. She had learned that this was different. The pack, as she called them, were akin to any other scavenging animal – individually cowardly, they drew courage from their numbers, and tended to pick on the weak. Show resistance, and they would back off. The trouble was that these weren't your usual scavengers. Their leaders were entitled rich kids, and denting their superiority complex was hard to do. Especially when Teresa started with so much they could pick on.

To them, she was the ideal target, and they never tired of taking pot shots at her. Over time, they had worn down her resistance, in the way that only prolonged bullying can. So this time she said nothing. Just fought back the tears with all her strength.

She would not give them the satisfaction.

Charging forward, she ploughed through the group of sneering faces, and shot along the corridor as fast as she could go.

The pack, scenting a chase, started after her, their jeering cries racing ahead of them. But as Teresa reached a bend in the corridor, she almost collided with a crewman coming the other way.

Sighting the pursuing pack, the crewman's gaze darted between Teresa's puffy, bloodshot eyes and the gleeful excited pleasure of the others. The crewman's expression turned cold. He stepped firmly between Teresa and the onslaught.

"That's enough. Go on, get out of here, all of you. Right now."

There was sullen muttering from somewhere in the group, but no one moved.

"I said, now! Unless you'd rather go on report?"

One of the taller boys, tossed his wavy brown hair and smirked. "I think, my father would have something to say about that. Don't you?"

In reply, the crewman raised his left arm, tapping the device fixed above his wrist. Everyone aboard Perseus had one: their very own Personal Data Assistant. What Teresa's friend Max had called "a more sophisticated iWatch". It was your own personal link to the ship's main computer, Aurora, and it could handle everything from messaging, managing schedules, interfacing with systems, you name it.

The crewman now pointed his PDA at each of the pack in turn, registering their ident tag. Once done, he folded his arms across his chest.

"We'll find out, won't we? 'Cos I've reported each of you for a behavioural infraction, and requested a schedule check to make sure you're not skipping any duties or classes you should be in right now."

Over her shoulder, Teresa saw the shuffled feet and sideways glances that shot around the pack, as the crewman went on. She carried on down the corridor as quietly as she could, hoping to slip away unnoticed. The crewman's words echoed in her wake.

"Now bugger off, unless you want me to call a guard!"

Teresa didn't stop until she reached the pool. It was her refuge: the one place she was sure to be alone. No one else enjoyed the pool as much as she did. In truth, it wasn't an actual pool – not a drop of water to be seen. It had been intended to be one of the many cargo holds, but their impromptu departure six years before had meant they had less supplies aboard, and subsequently more space available.

The suggestion to make Cargo Bay 17 into a zero gravity 'swimming pool' had been enthusiastically welcomed, and it proved very popular to begin with. But after all this time, the novelty had worn off, and few people ever bothered with it. That was one of its attractions for Teresa: the solitude. And, of course, it was the only place aboard she didn't need her chair.

Having locked the motorised chair into an anchor, she allowed herself to float freely into the pool. She laughed as she stretched and spun easily in the air, moving with a grace born of pure pleasure. Even though she'd now spent more years in her chair than out of it - and the only memories she possessed from before had little to do with running, jumping or swimming – to Teresa, there was no better experience than gliding about in zero-g.

She barely remembered the accident, though she had been known to wake from bad dreams about it over the years. What she remembered was the bright sunshine, her laughter, KC & the Sunshine Band on the radio, and her mother's smile. Sophia Petros had often smiled, and never more so than when with her daughter. The two had made quite a pair. "An enchanting sight", in her father's words. Both so full of life and happiness. Until the day they'd driven to the coast. Until that big 4x4 had lost control and ploughed into them, crumpling their own car, and ramming them off the road.

Sophia had never smiled again.

And Teresa had never walked again.

Her father, Travis, had changed that day too. He'd always said Sophia had a fire within her, and her death stoked a fierce blaze in his heart. The mission became all important, all consuming. He was still a caring father to Teresa, and raised her well. But he also ensured that, from a young age, she was involved in learning the ship's systems, their functions and operation. He intended her to become a valued member of the crew. Someone who had a real contribution to make.

Teresa had never minded his intentions. She'd always had a passion for science and a thirst for discovery. But Teresa's proud view of her father wasn't shared by everyone. Some of those aboard said he was too absorbed in the mission, obsessed by it. Power crazed, even. Of course, such things are always said about the rich. But when that man was Travis Petros - one of the richest oil millionaires in the world, and a technology tycoon to boot - the argument became more and more convincing.

With Perseus in-flight, the Ship's Captain, Arturo, actually commanded the mission now. But being an astronaut, rather than an organiser, some people still looked to Teresa's father to lead them. True, the idea was his, and he had recruited the people aboard, but it was always understood that he wouldn't command the mission. He simply wasn't qualified for that. But the wealthy patrons came to him with their complaints, and he became caught in the middle. If he did nothing, he would stir up resentment, and if he took action, he would overstep his boundaries. The wealthy didn't care about that: all they were interested in was getting their own way. But as Travis often said: "Four hundred people on one ship – that's a pressure cooker you don't want getting hot."

Sighing, Teresa flipped onto her back and used her arms to propel her as she began another turn about the pool.

Her father had been showing the strain recently. She always thought of him as the kind faced man he'd been when she was younger, whose strong arms could bring her such wonderful hugs, and who would put his world on hold for her lightest wish. Of course, Teresa knew there must be more to him than that. You don't get to be as wealthy as he was without being able to be serious. But her father had always managed to keep a divide between family time and work. Since coming aboard ship, he had done his best to make time for her, but there always seemed to be something he had to deal with. If not the rich passengers complaining, then the military causing arguments. Captain Arturo hadn't wanted to have military personnel on his ship, but Travis had been adamant that their skillset could be invaluable, and not only for self-defence.

Having been aboard Perseus with them for quite some time, Teresa wasn't sure they added much to the mix. Most of them were short tempered, and they didn't seem to appreciate being told what to do. By far the worst was Colonel Sylvester, their head guy. There were whispers that he wasn't actually a Colonel – he'd not been in the army for years - but that had been his rank, and he insisted on its use. He could be very mean. With flecks of grey in his hair, his head appeared to have been covered in salt and pepper, but his eyes were cold, and his mouth slid far too easily into a thin line. Teresa didn't like him much, and she doubted anyone else did either. He always thought he knew better than you, and wouldn't to listen to your ideas.

There was a lot of that going around. Even her dad didn't listen to her anymore. Not really.

It was a fortnight ago that she'd spotted it: a very small issue. So small that in day-to-day operation, it wouldn't be picked up, but as she was learning to run full system diagnostics, she'd been examining the operation as a whole. She had studied each component and its connections to rest of the system, and that was how she'd discovered it. There was a tiny error in the guidance calculations. It was roughly about 0.02% out in the calculations, a rounding error in the algorithm, not noticeable to direct flight, but if left unchecked, they could find themselves light years off course. Possibly too far out to be able to correct it. It might add who knew how long to the journey. What if they didn't have the supplies to make it?

Teresa had felt so proud: she'd found an error that no one else on the flight deck had. Finally, she was showing them how valuable she was. And what had happened? They ignored her. Patronised her. Treated her like a kid. The bridge crew weren't interested in what she'd found – her being a mere trainee - but she'd expected her mentor, Carlsson, to listen. A patient man, he'd always been impressed with her work and how quickly she grasped the often-complex tasks they had to do. But he dismissed her concerns too. He'd been nice about it, but still.

She'd burst into their cabin that night, launching a tirade at Travis as soon as she caught sight of him. What was the point in her having spent all that time learning the systems - training to be better, to be useful, to understand the ship's functions - if when it came to it, she was ignored?

Teresa ranted at her father until even he, usually the kindest person in the world to her, had snapped.

"Listen, mija, that's the way it is. Carlsson and the others have been working with those systems for far longer than you have, and they don't see a problem."

She'd exploded at this injustice. That was the point. They wouldn't look, but it was there. She'd seen it. Didn't he believe her? Travis had simply smiled at her and shrugged his shoulders.

"It doesn't matter what I think. This is your battle, for you to fight. If you want to." He'd laughed at that. "And if I know you, you will. Sometimes I think there's too much of your mother in you. She would never walk away from a fight either. Did I ever tell you the story of the time she got into a fight in a bar, when we were on a trip in California?"

"Oh, no, not *that* story again, please!" Teresa had rolled her eyes. "I know, papa. But they won't listen to me."

"Then there's only one way to fight. Show them. If you give them proof - evidence - they can't ignore that."

The old advice broke through her wandering thoughts. Teresa sat up, or as close to it as you could in in zero-g. Her eyes gleamed, and her jaw set firmly. The pack's words echoed in the back of her mind too, along with the disbelieving expressions of the bridge crew, but she'd show them. She'd show them all. She was worth ten of them, and they'd know it soon enough.

Teresa paddled back to her chair, and set off for her cabin, her mind a triumphant swirl of purpose.

She hardly noticed as she passed various crew members going about their duties. She was too preoccupied with how glorious it would be to have them all forced to admit she was right. Only as she approached their cabin did anything penetrate her victorious daydream, forcing her to halt. Raised voices echoed from inside. Her father's she recognised instantly, and it was the anger in his voice that stopped her. He was never angry. In all her life, Teresa could barely recall him shouting. Now, he sounded furious.

She tried to listen more closely to the second voice and work out its owner, but the cabin door opened with a jolt and Colonel Sylvester stamped out. He turned in the doorway, raising a finger.

"Mark my words, Petros. You are endangering the entire mission, even more so than you did launching early, without a full crew aboard."

Teresa heard her father's voice from within, a little quieter than it had been behind closed doors.

"You know perfectly well that was an impossible situation. You'd have waited, would you? Let the Government interfere and probably prevent us taking off at all?"

"*I'd* have fought. Held them off while we got all the supplies and people aboard possible. Then, we'd have been in the strongest position to launch with *all* the resources at our disposal. But I can't expect a *civilian* to understand the demands of command."

"What is that supposed to mean?"

Sylvester took a step back into the room. From her position, Travis' expression wasn't visible, but she saw his shoulders tense at Sylvester's approach.

"It means, Petros, that what this mission lacks is a strong leader. Arturo's not up to the job. He can't make the hard decisions when they need to be made. And I promise you one thing: I won't let this mission fail because of that."

Colonel Sylvester spun about, his lip curling at the sight of Teresa, and he stamped off down the corridor. Teresa hurried into the cabin and found her father sat at his desk, head in his hands.

"Papa? What was that about?"

Travis started at her voice. He rose quickly, trying to shape his mouth into a smile.

"Oh, nothing, mija. Nothing to worry about. Have you eaten? Do you want a drink?"

Teresa raised her eyebrows – an expression that clearly said, "yeah right". Turning at her lack of response, Travis saw it and sighed.

"You know, you look so much like your mother when you do that."

"And you'd tell her what's going on, so you can tell me."

Sighing again, Travis moved to a compartment where he took out a glass and poured himself a drink.

"Ok, ok. Well, you know why we're here, don't you?"

Travis sat down, and Teresa moved to join him. "Yes, of course, Papa. We're here to start over again."

Travis nodded.

"That's right. Over twenty years ago, I sat down with a group of people who felt the same as I did. We decided that the human race needed to find another planet to settle on, and do better. Not destroy the planet. Not hate, and fight, and kill each other over things that – when you come right down to it – don't actually matter. So, I found two very clever scientists, who designed Perseus for us."

Travis sighed again, and took a drink.

"The trouble is, this journey we're on is going to take longer than our lifespan, so it will be our descendants, our children's children, that finally arrive on the planet we chose."

Teresa tutted. "I know this part already."

"So, we had to find like-minded people, who would be committed to our cause, to make up our crew. This took a lot of time, and we had to be very careful. We didn't want the Government to find out."

"Because they'd try to stop you?"

"That's right. You see, mija, Governments are never happy when their people want to move outside their sphere of influence. This lessens their control, their power. And all government is about power. Don't believe anyone who tells you different."

Teresa nodded, and Travis smiled at her.

"Well, the Government did find out, and they raided our complex in Utah. I had to decide, in that moment, what we should do. Take off, even though we didn't have all the supplies and people we wanted, or stay and let the Government interfere."

"And you chose to go?"

"We had to, mija. This mission meant everything to your mother and I. We wanted to give you a better life, away from the Earth. People have poisoned it, and each other, with their prejudices, their hate, their ignorance and arrogance. We wanted something better for you: good people with a worthwhile goal. History has shown us so many examples of the love and wonderful acts humanity is capable of. We wanted that to be the foundation of a better way of life. And young people like you are the heart of that mission. You carry those values forward."

A spark of fervour burned in Travis's eyes, animating his entire face. Teresa cast her gaze down and stared unseeingly at her chair. Her mind was flooded with the pack's words again, rushing round and round her head. A cyclone of sneers, taunting her over and over.

"What is it, mija?"

He spoke softly, and waited patiently, until Teresa answered. There was a touch of hesitancy in her quiet words, and Travis had to move his head closer to hear.

"Not everyone here seems like that."

Travis shook his head.

"No. I'm sorry, mija, but some people aren't. And that is the cause of a lot of arguments aboard. A few got on board because their family helped to finance this venture, some because they have skill-sets we couldn't do without. And while they might agree with the principles, or the basic idea, they differ on the finer details. I can only hope that the community we build here will keep the core ideals of the mission alive."

Teresa raised questioning eyes to him.

"What about the soldiers?"

Travis laughed.

"They're actually here because I insisted that they could be useful members of the group." He rubbed the back of his neck. "I didn't bargain on Colonel Sylvester, though."

Teresa shot him a look, but Travis's warm smile brought a calming reassurance despite her concerns.

Her father waved a hand. "Don't worry about him. He talks big every now and then, but there's very little he can do. He's only one man. True, a grumpy, irritable man, but nothing to worry about."

Teresa remained silent. Perhaps her father was right, but she couldn't quite convince herself. Travis took her into his arms in a big, love-filled hug, and his warmth softened her resolve more and more.

"You're perfectly safe, mija. I won't let anything happen to you. I promise you that."

He kissed the top of her head, then put his hands on his hips. She watched him scowl his ridiculous scowl, waggling a joking finger at her.

"Now then, young lady. Shouldn't you be in bed? You've a shift on the flight deck in the morning."

Teresa couldn't help but laugh. She turned her chair and headed for her bunk, her chest considerably lighter than it had been.

The next morning, Teresa was up early to be sure she was on time for her work period. On her way to the flight deck she passed her friend Max, making his way to the mess hall after a night shift. He waved and called out to her.

"Meet me for lunch? I've got loads to tell you!"

She couldn't help grinning. Somehow, Max could always make her smile. He was such a fun guy, and his enthusiasm was infectious. It seemed to bubble over and engulf you.

"I'll be there."

Max beamed.

"Great. You won't believe my news. Seriously!"

He arched his eyebrows dramatically.

When she reached the flight deck, the usual compliment of people were there, with Carlsson supervising. His grey hair, pleasant smile and good humour always made her shifts enjoyable. Teresa was glad he was her mentor. His approach suited her.

As she moved to her allotted console, Teresa wished them all a good morning to little reaction. One or two grunted half-hearted responses, but otherwise she was greeted with silence. It seemed they had not forgotten her claims of a fortnight ago.

Carlsson, on the other hand, greeted her with his usual smile as she arrived beside him.

"Good morning, Teresa. Did you sleep well?"

"Yes, thank you."

"Excellent. Now, you know what you're doing?"

"Yes, Mr Carlsson."

"And what is that?"

"You wanted me to get to the bottom of the glitch in the air circulators in cargo hold 23."

"That's right. Remember, it's important we have a thorough working knowledge of all the ship's systems. It means we can fix, or easily identify the issues that maintenance have to deal with. Then crucial systems need only be down for the shortest time possible."

He winked and lowered his voice.

"And don't worry about them." He indicated the others with a jerk of the head. "They're all a little tense at the moment."

Teresa eyed him.

"Why?"

Carlsson chuckled.

"Oh, nothing you need worry about. Now, suppose you get on with those air circulators."

"Yes, Mr Carlsson."

Teresa bent her head to her task and worked busily. The problem, on the surface, seemed simple enough. The motor on the air circulator was stalling, and it was a simple job to reset it from the flight deck. But it was a recurring problem, so there had to be an underlying issue, and finding that was Teresa's assignment.

As she worked, she heard the others chatting at their consoles. Preston's voice carried across.

"Strange. There's a report of a disturbance in one of the holds on deck 50."

Barrett's disinterested reply echoed back.

"What's strange about that? Alert a guard and send them to investigate."

"That's the strange thing – I can't raise a guard. I'm getting no response on any channel."

Teresa hadn't realised that Carlsson had been earwigging too, until he took charge, quickly and calmly.

"Wong, run a system diagnostic. We may have to reboot comms. Barrett: be aware we may need you to route a message ship-wide via the PDAs that comms has encountered an issue."

"You got it."

"Wong, how's that diagnostic?"

Before Wong could reply, several figures burst onto the flight deck. Figures armed with guns. At their head was Colonel Sylvester, and as Carlsson began to ask what he thought he was doing, the Colonel brought his arm up and hammered the butt of his gun into Carlsson's face. Carlsson collapsed to the ground. A ripple of shock ran through the crew, but before any of them could move, Teresa shot towards Carlsson's prone form.

"What are you doing? Mr Carlsson, are you okay?"

She was aware of an arm reaching for her, but her only thought was to make sure Carlsson wasn't badly hurt. Reaching him, she found her mentor out cold, a savage red mark across his head where the gun butt had struck. She glared up at Colonel Sylvester, who showed his teeth in a smile, before training his gun on her. Teresa made to speak, but he cut her off.

"That's enough. No one else moves, and no one else gets hurt. This is a mutiny."

Several hours later, a deadlock was reached. Captain Arturo had attempted to negotiate, but having barricaded themselves in the flight deck, Colonel Sylvester and the military held all the cards. Though their diplomacy skills lacked finesse, as they resorted to threatening to shut down life support all across the ship if their demands were not met.

The Colonel was only prepared to accept their surrender, and immediate recognition of his supreme authority in command of the mission. Arturo was not prepared to offer this. That was where their talks stalled.

Trapped on the flight deck, Teresa felt her chest tighten with every breath. The crew around her seemed determined to avoid eye contact with anyone, in case they accidentally provoked their captors. For their part, the military appeared on edge too, jaws clamped shut, and their knuckles white as they gripped their guns. Perhaps they hadn't expected to find themselves in a drawn-out hostage situation today any more than she had.

At the central console, Colonel Sylvester paced. His every step thumped the deck like a hammer. Teresa had never seen his mouth draw such a thin line, and his glare was so dark that even his own men gave him a wide berth. To Teresa, he appeared the human equivalent of a volcano: ready to erupt at any moment.

Strangely, she found she didn't care.

"So, what are you going to do now?"

Everyone on the flight deck held their breath as she spoke. One or two made small shushing gestures, but she ignored them, and carried on.

"Or are we all going to just sit here, until someone gives in?"

Carlsson reached out to restrain her, but she shook him off. He'd come around during the negotiations and, once her concern for her mentor's welfare had been assuaged, Teresa had begun to find the whole situation absurd. She'd quickly lost any patience she had with the mutineers. Some of them were clearly uncomfortable even being there, and Teresa had had ample time to make her mind up about Colonel Sylvester. He was a bully. Plain and simple. This time, she wouldn't keep quiet, wouldn't put up with the idea that she, or anyone else here, deserved to be treated this way. Some fights were too important to let slide.

She fixed the Colonel with a hard stare. "If that's your plan, I can tell you now, it won't work. Besides, there's a whole other issue that you haven't even considered."

Carlsson leant over and spoke across her. "Teresa, please, don't antagonise them. It isn't wise."

Teresa clocked the relief crossing the faces of those nearby, particularly Major Winston's. He was second in command of the military forces aboard Perseus, and his involvement in the mutiny had shocked Teresa almost more than anything else that day. She had always thought him so… nice. Easily the kindest of the soldiers, he'd always behaved like a decent, reasonable man. Such an act seemed out of character for him. It only proved that you couldn't judge by appearances alone. She could only trust herself here.

In her silence, Carlsson began to relax his breathing. But then, Colonel Sylvester spoke, his voice a soft and menacing purr.

"You're right, my dear. In fact, Miss Petros, *you* might be the solution."

He marched to the comms unit with sharp strides, and addressed himself to the rest of the ship.

"Arturo, I know you can hear me. I'll give you five minutes to surrender and accept my terms, or you will be responsible for the death of Miss Petros."

Teresa's brain froze. She couldn't process what she'd heard. Her veins felt as though they'd just been flooded with ice, as a chill ran right through her body. She only half-listened as the Colonel continued.

"Petros enjoys pulling strings for his own gain. Well, now he can pull them for mine. And don't waste time: this is not a negotiation. You have four minutes, fifty-five seconds, remaining."

Colonel Sylvester turned away from the comms unit with a broad, thin smile. Teresa was dimly aware of every eye on the bridge riveted on her, but she didn't move or speak. Her stomach seemed to have dropped away, leaving only emptiness inside. There was nothing she could do, and her father couldn't help her. He was out there, and she in here.

With the Colonel and his gun.

Biting her lip hard, she fought to keep the fear and panic shooting through her from spreading to her face. She tried to think clearly, but she couldn't. She didn't want to die.

She wanted to live, and that was all that really mattered. And to think, how she'd been so worked up about the pack and their stupid, meaningless words. All that trouble over the algorithm problem, about being right and proving everyone wrong. What did any of that matter now?

But even as those questions swirled in her head, she could hear her father's voice, in one of his many reminders about the importance of their mission. All it had meant to her mother, and his vow to complete it for her. To give Teresa the best life he could.

She knew what she had to do.

Teresa had to swallow twice before her voice worked. There was a slight tremor still, but it gathered strength with every word.

"Errr… we have a bigger problem than who's in charge."

Sylvester ignored everyone else on the bridge. Fixing an unwavering gaze on her, he gestured an invitation.

"Please, go on. I suppose you should have a last request."

"I found it the other day: a tiny error in the navigation calculations. It's only small, but it could put us light years off course if it's not fixed..."

She trailed off to silence under the Colonel's stare. She wasn't sure that she liked what was working behind those dark eyes of his. After a moment, he snapped at Barrett.

"Check it."

Barrett began to protest, but when the Colonel fingered his gun, the crewman hurried to comply. There were a few moments of silence while Barrett worked, then everyone jumped as someone banged on the flight deck door. The muffled voice of Travis could be heard outside. Teresa's heart froze at the sound.

"Sylvester, let me in. I'm alone and unarmed. I just want to talk."

Teresa's eyes went wide and round as they focussed on the sealed door. The Colonel's face contorted into a snarl as he barked at Major Winston.

"Let him in. If he's lying, shoot him."

Teresa tried to keep her expression level as the door opened. Travis smiled that warm smile she knew so well as he entered, hands raised.

"See? No tricks."

There was no returned smile from the Colonel. He only sneered at Travis.

"What do you want?"

"I want to try and end this peacefully. We're all on the same side here, so why don't we put the guns down and talk?"

"We? WE?! There's no 'we' here, Petros. Only you and us. And I know what you're about. Restart humanity? A better blueprint? No. This is all about making you a God, a saviour, and I won't die for that. Do you hear me?!"

He took a step towards Travis, and Teresa could hold it no longer. She cried out and Sylvester spun to face her so fast that she recoiled in her chair.

"Yes, that's what your dearest dad wants to do here. That's all any of the rest of us are good for, to help him bask in his own glorious reflection. I'm the only person who sees through his lies."

"It's okay, mija." Travis moved forward slowly, putting himself between them. "Leave her alone, Sylvester. If you've a problem, I'm right here. You talk to *me*."

"You don't give me orders!"

The Colonel was practically screaming. Lines of fury were etched into his face so deep that they might have been carved there. A vein throbbed on the side of his neck.

"Do you understand me?! You do NOT give me orders. Do you know who I AM? Do you?!"

He stepped right up to Travis, bawling in his face like a Drill Sergeant. Travis held his ground. His silence seemed to infuriate Sylvester all the more.

"ANSWER ME!"

For a heartbeat, there wasn't a sound. No one moved. Teresa didn't dare breathe. Then Travis spoke. He didn't shout. He wasn't angry. He spoke quietly and calmly into the vacuum. His voice seemed to carry around the room by sheer force of personality.

"I know who you are. I think I've known for a long time, but I hoped things wouldn't come to this. I hoped others would recognise you for what you are, and that they would come together for the sake of each other and deal with you. I see now, I was wrong. I should never have allowed a tyrant like you aboard in the first place. That was my mistake, and for that, I'm sorry."

Into the ringing hush that followed, every soul could hear Sylvester's rabid breaths as he took in Travis's cool expression. He whispered in a voice filled with hate.

"No, *this* was your mistake."

The gunshot rang around the flight deck, echoing a hundred times louder than it was. Teresa screamed as Travis buckled to the deck. She tried desperately to get to him, but Carlsson held her back.

Sylvester turned on her, gun still in his hand. A savage delight filled his face as he took aim, but a second shot burst through his chest before he could reach for the trigger again. He fell beside Travis as, beyond them both, Major Winston lowered his pistol.

"No more deaths today."

Teresa was not aware of the silence in the room, nor of the expressions of mingled horror and shock on the faces around her. All she could hear were her own hysterical, agonised tears as she stared at her father's body. Her whole body crumpled as she was lost to the pain. A numbing, sickening pain, and a despair so deep that it was all Teresa knew.

It was a long time before she felt anything else.

Sylvester's death was the end of the mutiny. Winston took charge, and had the military stand down and surrender their weapons.

The peace that followed enabled the conflicts to be discussed around a table, and the result was that a Councillor position was created with an elected representative from within the crew taking the role. It would be their job to make decisions alongside Captain Arturo, and to ensure all views were heard, and that such a tragedy was never repeated in the future.

It took Teresa quite some time to recover from her father's death. Having lost both parents in tragic circumstances, there was concern amongst others that she might lose faith in the mission. But, as Travis Petros had said many times, Teresa had her mother's spirit. There was a fierce, indomitable fire inside her.

Teresa surprised many by excelling in her apprenticeship, displaying a far greater knowledge of the ship's systems than her counterparts. Carlsson was very proud of her, and she quickly gained the respect of her colleagues through her excellent work ethic and strong character. Despite fears to the contrary, she remained dedicated to the mission, perhaps even more so than she had been while her father was alive. She was truly grateful to have her friend Max there to support her through the hard times, but to this day, she rarely discusses her father.

Max encouraged Teresa to hold a memorial service for Travis, which has subsequently been held every year since, and is always well attended by the majority of the crew. They remain firm friends.

Teresa was also found to be partially vindicated in her findings, as Carlsson, investigated her claims more deeply and discovered a rounding error in her PDA's readout. Hence no one else agreeing with her findings.

Today she is a fully-fledged member of the bridge crew. Very much her father's daughter, she is as respected among the crew as he was, for her honesty and integrity. A woman he would be proud of.

Her new PDA has the ident: **mija**.

Alec James originates from Wales, where the magnificence of the landscape inspired him to put pen to paper at an early age. He now resides in Chester writing poetry, plays, murder mysteries, short stories and has even tried his hand at a novel or two. When not chained to his keyboard, Alec enjoys treading the boards under the bright lights of the theatre, rocking out to very different audiences in one of his three bands, and running for his life from hordes of marauding zombies. It his stated intention to one day live in an art deco house Poirot's set designer would be proud of, own his own Triumph Thunderbird, and to have a cat. He's refused to be drawn on which of these is the most achievable goal.

School Strike For Baby Hope

David Thorpe

I never thought of myself as a hero.

I'd had the baby three months and everyone was still on about the same thing like a looping gif.

"You're too young."

"Why'd you keep it?"

Wish I'd had a fiver for each time I heard that.

My mum was always ranting about how I was missing school. "Huh. Never expected any daughter of mine to make the same mistake I did."

Well that's her fault isn't it? Going around complaining about being a grandmother at 36 as if all that mattered was what other people thought of her.

First time I took Hope to school everyone gathered round, making a fuss. You'd think they'd never seen a baby before. Treating me like I was from outer space, like I was no longer one of them.

"Isn't she gorgeous?"

"Does breastfeeding hurt?"

"You smell of gone-off milk and dirty nappies." (He couldn't have smelt me 'cause he was too far away due to social distancing... could he?)

"I wish I didn't have to come to school. Wait–" Rapid shaking of head. "But I don't want a baby."

'Cept Anneka. She was loyal. "Shut up you lot. Give her space."

She pushed 'em back to let Hope breathe. Mind you she hates Pete too. That's the dad.

As she walked me away from the school gate she let out how she was going on a demo. "We're not going to school on Friday. Hey, Evie, seeing as you're not going to school anyway why don't you join us? Here, look at this."

She showed me a YouTube video about how the world was going to end because people were driving too many cars and flying.

Hope was grizzling and I put her over my shoulder and stroked her back. "It's just a video. Probably made up. You know what the internet's like."

"Just listen to what the girl says," she said. "By the time your little Hope's your mum's age, if we don't do anything all the ice caps'll be slush puppies, London'll be ten feet underwater, and if there's anybody left we'll all be fighting over the last bar of chocolate."

"So what? That's not my problem. I've got my hands full." Literally, as it happened at the time since I couldn't afford a buggy. I was starting to smell something coming from her lower end. "I'm knackered half the time, and the rest of the time I've got to take care of 'er. You'll get it when you're in the club yourself."

"Suit yourself. Anyway take this to read." She stuffed a magazine between me and Hope and ran off.

I trotted home as fast as I could to change her nappy.

After she'd finally fallen asleep in my arms later that night I opened the paper. It looked well scary to me. They was all on about being arrested and chaining themselves to gates.

One article caught my eye – it was about Gandhi and Nelson Mandela. We'd done them in school. They made the world a better place. For a while, at least. I liked Nelson's twinkly eyes.

That night my mum picked another argument while I was bathing her. Just 'cos I'd left a nappy on the floor for five minutes. "Hey you. I'm fed up with cleaning after your nappies. Why don't you get Pete to come round and make himself useful?"

"He doesn't want owt to do with it, you know that. 'Sides, he'd only make things worse," I yelled back.

"Pity he didn't think of that at the time," she said. "Men. They're all the same. Live in the moment. Never think of the future."

"That's not true," I said. "What about Gandhi and Nelson Mandela?"

"Yeah, we could do with a few of them around here, no mistake," she said. "But there's never one around when you need one, is there?"

Next day I was sorting out Hope's cot when Anneka messaged. "Well, you coming then?"

"You're joking," I texted. "What, get arrested? With Hope?"

"Don't be daft. No one's going to be arrested. We're just going to stand outside the school and hand out leaflets."

"In the pouring rain? Have lots of fun."

"Suit yourself. But it's your future. And Hope's."

I wished she wouldn't keep bringing my child into this. I texted back: "No one knows what's going to happen. Just look at the pandemic. No one predicted that."

Right back it came: "Did actually. They said climate change is likely to cause more of them. Problem is nobody takes any notice. 'Cause they're all old. That's why we're doing this."

I sent a dunno emoji.

She sent me a link to a website. I didn't have time to click on it, and I don't like people pushing their ideas onto me either.

Two minutes later she sent: "I need you there or it's just me vs. Nita. She'll be going on and on about her new tattoo. C'mon, we can have a laugh."

Later, as I was feeding Hope, she looked so happy, gurgling away. Her little mouth and sparkly eyes. So innocent. Like she could do anything in her life.

I guessed I must have looked like that once, when my mum had me. Wonder what was going through her head then? Not that she'd tell me now.

Things don't turn out the way you expect, do they?

I never thought enough about the future before.

Now look at me.

I burped her and she was sick on my shoulder. Should've put a flannel there. Stupid, now my jacket's got to go to the dry cleaner's. More expense.

See what I mean?

When I had a moment I finally plucked up the balls to call Pete. 'Course he didn't answer. So I nicked my mum's phone and used that 'cause I knew he wouldn't have her number and know it was me. He answered on the third ring.

"What?"

"Don't hang up. It's me, Evie. Will you babysit for me?"

"Oh it's you. I told you I don't want–"

"If you don't do it I'll tell Charlene about Hope and that you're a selfish wanker who only cares about one thing."

He snorted. "She wouldn't care, coming from you. She'll say you deserved it."

"You've got a lot to learn about women. We stick together."

"Yeah like cold pudding."

"Well what about it? Come on, you owe me."

Silence for a bit, then: "When is it?"

"Friday. Morning."

"No can do. Got a dental appointment."

"Really?"

"Yeah. Straight up. Find some other sucker."

The line went dead. Great. I phoned another mate a year older who'd left school already.

"Why'd you want babysitting at that time?" she wanted to know. "Where are you going?"

"None of your business, is it? Just tell me yes or no. I'll pay you. Not much, but…"

"I won't do it if you won't tell me."

"Okay if it's that important. It's no big deal but there's a protest about climate change."

She grunted. "In that case no way. You want to put my dad out of a job?"

"Why, what's he do?"

"Works in the petrol station. Electric cars don't need petrol or diesel. What's he going to do for a living if you lot get your way?"

"It's not my lot, and I didn't make global warming did I? I'm just going on a demo."

"Forget it, soz."

And she hung up. No Nelson Mandela her neither.

So I didn't have no choice. Friday morning there was me and Hope slung round my neck in a sling, hopping around outside the school, plastic bag to keep the rain off her, feeling guilty 'cause it wasn't a bag for life, but are they waterproof?

"Here you are." Charlene shoved a placard into my spare hand. I held it so I could read its message: "Stop Burning My Future!"

We was all social distancing and wearing masks, standing in a line on the pavement. There was a lot of us out. Mark, Rasheed, Benji, Chloe. They smiled at me and, 'cause they'd been told not to this time, they didn't come too near to the baby.

"Aw, isn't he cute?"

"She. It's a girl. I just don't want to dress her in pink."

"Right," said Rasheed.

"Gender stereotyping."

"Yeah, 'course," said Chloe with Instagram eyelashes so long you could sweep the floor with them.

When all the buses and the parents dropping their kids off had gone, because not everybody in school was striking, there was just the odd car coming by. Other people's placards read, in hand-painted messages, "Citizens Assemble!" and "School Strike For The Planet" and "Emergency! There's No Planet B!".

They whooped and sang songs. I didn't know the words, but I got caught up in it, it was infectious. Soon I was yelling too, whenever a car drove by. It was fun. Some hooted and we cheered, and some guys made obscene gestures out of the windows and we booed.

Then this photographer turned up. He started asking questions, like why were we here, what did we think? Homed in on me and Hope. "Ah. Photogenic," he went. "My editor will like this."

Snap. Snap. Snap. "You're not at school are you?" he asked me.

I kept my head down, thinking I must look like something the cat dragged in. Having kids is not good for your appearance. I mumbled vague words at him and then Hope saved me by starting her wheedling.

Time for a feed. I said my goodbyes to everyone. "Sorry. Can't stay any longer. Can't feed her out here in the rain you know?"

I left the reporter and walked down the line along the pavement. They all thanked me for coming. I was surprised how good I felt. It was nice to see everyone. I was glad to be doing something, out of the house.

I kept quiet about it to Mum.

Next morning, even before I got up – we'd had a sleepless night, what with Hope waking me up every five minutes – she was shouting up the stairs again. "Hoi. Teenage mum. Get your fancy pants down here!"

Huh, what have I done now? I thought. Put on my dressing gown, left Hope sleeping in her cot.

"Look. You're only on the front page." She showed me the local paper as I filled the kettle. "Don't normally buy it but the neighbour told me."

Next to an advert for kitchens and a headline about a new road there was a big photo of me and Hope, all wet and bedraggled, and behind us Anneka holding up a poster with that Greta Thunberg on it. And a headline: Teenage mum strikes for the future.

Mum was like "What, so you an anarchist now?"

I pushed past her to plug the kettle in. "Don't be daft. Do you believe everything you read in the papers?"

"Photos don't lie," she said. "I don't want no daughter of mine getting a criminal record."

"It's just a school demo, Mum. I was only there for an hour. Hardly a bank robber am I?"

"They should be in classes not striking." She headed back into the kitchen. "Learn something proper instead of skiving off."

Yeah, like she never skived off in her life.

I was just getting on with my Saturday, and wondering if they'd be doing the strike next Friday, when the phone pinged. "Hey. You'll never guess what?" – Anneka.

"What?" I texted.

"The telly want to talk to you."

"???"

"BBC's seen your picture in the paper and want a follow-up."

"No way. That's mental."

"Yeah, but cool. Right?"

I didn't text back. Five minutes later I got an actual call.

"What? Don't you wanna?"

"I dunno. What would I say?" I asked her. "I don't know squat about climate change."

She put on a pleading voice. "You've got to do this, Evie. They don't want to speak to any of the rest of us. It's 'cos you've got a baby."

"Yeah but you know what happens to people on the telly. They get all kinds of grief."

"Come on. Ple-ease. It's our chance to get some real publicity. It's for the planet, Evie."

"I only went along 'cause you said so."

"Chill, sis. Just say what you feel. I'll come with you if you like."

"I'm not sure."

"Deal then. Ok?"

I got collywobbles straightaway. I'd only 27 hours to prep for it.

When Hope finally nodded off I did some frantic googling on my phone. Videos would be easiest to learn from but it was too much data so I had to do some reading. Here was a website about the school strike with some cool graphics. Plenty of photos of protests at other schools, crowds of kids looking really passionate and yelling with banners and stuff. I couldn't hardly think of me being one of them. They all looked like they knew what they were doing.

But one banner stuck out for me – 'Why Should We Grow Up In A World That's Dying?' I continued reading. I read while suckling Hope and I read in bed. If nothing else I was determined to memorise 1.5° and 10 years. 1.5° and 10 years. I repeated it over and over in my head until I fell asleep.

On waking I checked my appearance again. I looked shit. Stretchmarks, bags under my eyes, needed a haircut. I made sure to put pads over my nipples under my bra so no milk seeped through. That wouldn't be a good look. Desperately sought out a clean top. Tried to make the best of my hair. Arggh! Why wouldn't it go straight? And my skin! It seemed to have changed so none of my make-up worked.

I dressed Hope in a nice green babygrow. She looked gorgeous, as ever.

I had no money so they sent a cab to pick me up. That felt posh. Never been in a cab before.

Remember. 1.5° and 10 years. 1.5° and 10 years.

Anneka was at the studio already. The place was a bit shoddy to be honest. Not what I expected, glamorous, like. They did their best to make me feel relaxed, gave me a coffee, but the collywobbles were back. I needed the loo. 1.5° and 10 years. Right up to the last moment I was saying to Anneka – "You do it. It was your idea. Please!"

But the reporter wasn't interested in her.

"Just remember Mandela," whispered Anneka. "Do you think he asked to go to jail or be a leader? It's what happens when you stand up for what you believe in. You do believe in it don't you?"

I looked at Hope's face, so peaceful sleeping there, in my

sling. Not minding all the fuss going on around and the bright lights. "I suppose so. Yeah."

"Then just be yourself. Speak from your heart."

Heart. Right.

The lights were too bright. The reporter smiled. She looked smaller than on our screen. She began by asking me why I was doing this.

I took a gulp of air. "I want to know my daughter can have at least as good a future as, like, my mum had." (I thought I'd better get my Mum in there.)

The reporter nodded. She wanted more words.

"I'm doing it because Hope won't be able to live under water when the sea level's risen, and 'cause she ought to be able to see real live polar bears and elephants and tigers, and don't you think she shouldn't have to tell her children that they all died out before they were born?"

The reporter nodded. Then she asked me a trick question. At least I thought it was a trick. I didn't even understand it. Something about parts per million in the air.

I'd run out of words. I forgot all about 1.5° and 10 years.

I wasn't going to be fazed though. Think heart, I said to myself.

Hope woke up and gave us her best smile.

Everyone in the studio let out a collective sigh. To be honest, I did too.

I saw her, ten or fifteen years from now, old enough to know.

I saw her screaming while outside the house floodwaters raged past and burst into our living room.

I saw her crying as the last tree in the Amazon was felled.

I heard her yelling at me as we watched food riots at the supermarket, clutching empty bags and empty tummies. "Why did you let me be born? Why didn't you do something? You must've known!"

I blinked, and her smile was back, aimed right at me.

I wanted her to keep this smile. It was the most precious thing in the world.

I looked the reporter right in the eye and said, "I don't know much about the science, but I do know one thing. As a mother. It's stupid not to think of the future."

David Thorpe came up with the Marvel Universe Earth-616. His prize-winning YA SF novel Hybrids was called "stunningly clever" by The Times. He co-founded the London Screenwriters Workshop and has taught 1000s of hours of script and creative writing, and published a how-to book on the subject. YA climate fiction novel Stormteller led to his presence on the first two Hay Literature Festival climate fiction panels. He's worked on a number of short films and written a dozen books and 1000s of journalistic articles on environmental sustainability and renewable energy, including One Planet Cities: sustaining humanity within planetary limits and The One Planet Life. He is director of the One Planet Centre CIC and lives in south Wales near his favourite bookshop, The Dragon's Garden.

Crimson Constellations

Abby Mayers and Melody Lumb

Squinting into the silence of the dimly lit corridor, Mable shifted her weight from one aching sole to the other. She'd been standing in line with only the back of a stranger for company for what felt like an age. Unable to turn around and see the many others standing sentinel, the pounding of her heart filled her ears. Her head was still caught in a loop of questions. Why had she abandoned her natural logic, which had never thus far faltered? The spontaneity of it all made her stomach twist, but there was no way to back out of the decision now. She'd signed her name. With a sudden shuffling of feet and the disappearance of a nameless figure into a side door, she was one step closer.

A yawn crept up on her. She'd been picking up extra shifts where she could between studying, and the ache plagued her every muscle. That's what had driven her to do this stunt, but now that she was waiting, about to face a procedure that hadn't undergone her rigorous scrutiny, or that of any acclaimed scientist, the doubts came creeping in. Despite how much her father would deny it, money was still sparse, five years on from the economic crisis of 2020, and his bakery never seemed to bring in enough to cover their small family of three. She wanted – needed – to do something, she couldn't be the reason that her little brother went hungry again. The door swung open a second time and another masked stranger was drawn away. Another step closer.

Temptation had never beckoned Mable like this before. The gift of a clear-cut conscience had always saved her before she blurted 'yes'. As for the money, she'd sneak it into the bakery's cash register when her father wasn't looking. He would never object to some extra cash, as long as he didn't know where it had come from. Mable couldn't bear to put him through any more embarrassment. As much as he tried to hide it, it was blatantly obvious: they needed help. All of this required the art of deception, something Mable was less than practiced in. She'd simply never needed to lie before, not to her father, her brother or her girlfriend – well, apart from the odd white lie.

Another swing of the ominous side door, another pace forward. Against the chipped paint and ancient peeling posters with polite requests to keep distance and wear masks, the fluorescent poster had jumped out to Mable in the dank alleyway which had remained the same for as long as she could remember. After skim-reading its contents, the only thing that had remained in her memory was the number at the bottom. It was a sum larger than anything she had seen before, and now it was just within her grasp, but it came with a price. She'd have to step out of the safety net her father had provided for her, in order to provide him with a net of his own. Without giving many details, the poster had briefly stated the date and location of the transaction, and what her role to play would be.

They called it a chip, and it would be inserted onto the optic nerve to alter the vision, giving the individual the ability to see The Virus. Whether this was safe, or even possible, had only crossed her mind after she hadrun to the location and hastily signed her name.

Lost in a chain of frantic thought, she hadn't realised that she was at the front of the queue. The rush ofjittery nerves sprung through her veins, adrenalin making her vision sharpen. Her pulse raised. Her hands grew clammy.

The door to her right swung open, spilling light into the shadowy corridor, and Mable was beckoned in. Blinking in the harsh change of lighting above, the room solidified to reveal a plain, stark-white space. Strong chemical smells made her wince as her eyes fell upon a metal bed, which stood in the middle of the room, covered with a thin sheet.

A tall figure clad in protective dress strode towards the table, a document in hand, voice deep as they said, "Sit down."

Mable followed without hesitation, dread settling in her stomach. The smooth coolness of the table made herhair stand on end, her back uncomfortable against its unforgiving surface.

The man's voice came from her left, along with sounds of metal and plastic clicking into place. "You'll haveto rest before you see the effect take place, then you will send your report back to us weekly. Understood?"

She nodded, mute with apprehension."Alright, this will hurt. Don't move."

Out of the corner of her eye, she saw him move towards her and scrunched her eyes closed tight. Before she could register what was happening, she felt a metallic chill on her temple, and she gasped in a shuddering breath.

Several things happened in very quick succession; an ear-splitting crack, a sharp shooting pain across her temple, a blinding flash of red. The searing pain subsided almost instantly, leaving Mable with a throbbing sensation, and as she peeled her eyes open, her vision blurred and her head spun.

The earth tilted precariously as she tried to sit up. She gasped air into her lungs and blinked in an attempt to regain some balance. The man grabbed her arm to steady her, but she yanked it away.

"I'm fine." She succeeded at standing this time, although she was still swaying slightly. As her head gave a harsh stab of pain, her hand flew by instinct to touch where the chip had been inserted, and she found asmall bead of blood. A tissue was pressed into her hand, and Mable glanced to look up into the face of the man. "Can I have the money now?"

He sighed. "Yes, but if you're still groggy I'm not supposed to let you leave."

"I'm fine." She shifted her posture as if to prove her point. He stared at her for a second, then turned around and leaned over a locked box. He returned with a thick envelope and laid it in her hand.

"What are you planning on doing with all this? You're too young to be in need of this kind of money."

"Everyone needs this kind of money." She turned to leave, but spared a moment to face him again. "Thank you."

A bell trilled as Mable entered the bakery. Sliding the key out of the door and locking it again after herself, she surveyed the dim room.

The familiar low hum of the oven emanated from the back room, where her father was presumably preparing for tomorrow morning. The aroma of freshly baked bread drifted through the house and greeted Mable with its welcoming scent. In spite of this, she checked behind her before sneaking to the cash register. She took a few notes from the envelope hidden in her coat and placed them in the till, then continued through to the kitchen.

Attempting to go unnoticed, she spotted Emmi perched on the worktop in her sage-green knitted jumper, swinging her legs in a blur of brightly-coloured tights. Her laughter rang through the cramped room, no doubt at one of Mable's dad's terrible jokes. Josh was covered almost head-to-toe in flour as usual, kneadingdough next to Emmi, who caught Mable's eye as she entered.

"Hey you." Emmi smirked, "I thought I'd have mastered the art of baking before you finally turned up." Josh glanced over his shoulder, smiling softly. "The day you master baking will be the day I retire, Emmi."

He clapped the flour from his hands before turning to his daughter fully, "So honey, where've you been?I've never heard Jupiter pester so much. Then this one turns up looking for you," he chuckled.

Thinking fast for an excuse, Mable blurted, "Tampons!" Josh's face turned scarlet. "I – um – needed some,you know... that time of the month."

"Okay, okay I get it." Josh surrendered, shuffling back to his dough. Mable nodded to the stairs and Emmi sprung from her perch to follow.

"I'll bring something up for you in a bit!" Josh shouted after them as they began the ascent to Mable'sbedroom.

Mable threw herself down on the bed, an arm hung over her eyes. The pounding in her head hadn't stopped."Tired?" Emmi guessed, sprawling out next to her girlfriend.

Mable only hummed in confirmation which turned into a squeal as a black ball of fur leaped onto her. "Margot, stop it!" She yelled between bursts of laughter as she attempted to subdue her energetic dog. Margot eventually settled between them.

Closing her eyes, Mable buried her head into the dog's fur. She felt a warm hand drawing rhythmic circles into her back.

"This isn't like you, Mae. What's up?"

"Oh, I'm just tired." She looked over with the brightest smile she could muster. Cropped sandy hair fallingto frame her face, Emmi grinned back, her forest-green eyes twinkling as they always did, the crease on her forehead deepened.

"Really I'm fine, it's just a headache." Mable felt heat flood to her face, hating having to lie. No, she wasn't lying, she *did* have a headache, but it felt so much bigger than that, like she'd changed somehow in the few short hours that had passed. Emmi didn't need to know; she was bound to worry, and there was no need. What she didn't know couldn't hurt her.

"Alright." Emmi's head tilted in concentration, as if Mable was a puzzle she was trying to solve, "but you'd tell me if something was up, wouldn't you?"

Swallowing hard, Mable forced herself not to look away from Emmi's eyes, like pools of green, "Yeah, of course."

Mable didn't know how long they lay there, listening to their synchronised steady breaths, having shifted so that Mable's head rested against Emmi's chest. Emmi's hand methodically traced infinity across Mable's back, pressing gentle kisses on her dark hair. It gave a greater sense of peace between the swathes of fatigue that washed over her, lulling Mable into a dreamless sleep.

With a jolt, Mable awoke to the cold evening air drifting in through the open window, the gentle, distantsigh of waves lapping against the rocks. She peered through the glass and saw the first orange rays of sunset glimpsing from behind the clouds. After flinging back the sage jumper that had been draped atop of her and folding it to be returned to Emmi, she swung her legs over the cold side of the bed. Her drowsiness vanished as she realised that the thick envelope from the morning was still in her pocket. She removed it and stashed it underneath her mattress, then set out as if nothing had happened.

Across the hallway lay her little brother's bedroom door, covered with plastic stars. She flung it open. "Buddy, are you coming to the beach?" she said breathlessly.

Jupiter nodded, his dark curls bouncing on his head, almost covering his eyes. He mocked her tone, "I've been waiting for you, *buddy*."

Storming down the stairs, she grabbed Margot's lead as Jupiter wound a red woollen scarf around his neck.

They walked in silence until they rounded the corner to the beach. As soon as the ocean air hit her face, Mable could breathe deeply again. She felt as though nothing else mattered. Not the chip, not The Virus - only her brother, her dog and the deep red sun resting on the horizon, reflecting on the softly rolling waves. They slowed their pace as they tread the sand that would bear no evidence of their venture by morning.

It was Jupiter who broke through the rhythm of the waves and the cry of the gulls, "Today was boring without you."

"Flattered, but didn't you have school work to keep you entertained?"

Jupiter rolled his eyes and, far from his usual happy-go-lucky attitude, he sighed deeply. "It only took halfan hour. I could do this stuff years ago. I want something new that's more difficult. I'm tired of sitting in myroom staring at the ceiling."

"I know bud, I'm sorry, but that's just how it is. You know you can't go out, it's not safe. Imagine howmuch worse it would be if we were in the city. Look at the waves, the sun, there's no loud traffic or skyscrapers – it's nice, don't you think? And you're safe here, that's all that matters." Mable repeated the spiel she'd said hundreds of times over in an attempt to persuade Jupiter that he had all he needed in this small seaside village. But there was still no dulling his ambition for adventure. He stopped their progress up the beach to gaze longingly out at the wide expanse of his uncharted world.

"I know it's boring for you. I get it, but-"

Cutting her off, his small frame shaking with the force of his sobs that tore through his chest, "No, you don't.You don't get any of this. I can't do anything. I'm stuck here - locked in the house, allowed out once a day like some kind of pet, but I'm not, okay? I need more than four walls and piles of books. I need more than knowledge without being able to use it for anything. You can't understand how frustrating this is for me to only ever see the sun going down on another day that I've wasted away. I'm grateful, really, for you and dad trying to keep me safe. Except I'm only existing now. I need to live, and to do that I need to find... to find something more than this." He sighed again, his expression softening, but still looking far older than his years. "But I'm scared, Mable. I know I can't do all these things I wish I could do, because I'm scared. I know that The Virus could kill me, because of my stupid, no-good, weak lungs. I just wish it were all different, and that I could live before I die." He looked up at his sister, tears in his eyes, and she held him in her arms and kissed his nest of curly hair.

"I know, buddy. I know."

She didn't know what else to say. Should she tell him about the chip? If it worked, she could take him places and still protect him from The Virus. But that was a big 'if'. She couldn't give him false hope, couldn't see the sparkle re-appear in his eyes only to take it away again if she realised the chip didn't work. It was all too uncertain. All she could do was hold him tighter and tighter still to her chest, as if to singlehandedly bar all his hurt, and all the hurt in the world.

She wanted so badly to take him out of here. To explore the world that had only lived in books, the people, the places, the adventure that promises more than this mundane routine which doesn't lead anywhere. Butthe memories flooded back, of the time that she had ventured out into a world so different to the only one she had ever known.

Buildings had stretched higher than she had ever seen. As masked people bustled around her, immersed in their own lives as they instinctively followed arrows painted onto the pavement, she gripped her father's hand tightly. The black van had appeared from nowhere. Everyone's heads snapped towards it as it screeched to a halt at the side of the busy street, where three people exited in full protective outfits. They hadadvanced on an unknowing woman who, upon noticing their eyes trained on her, stumbled backwards in a futile attempt of escape. But not before they seized her and led her, struggling, into the back of the van.

Mable hadn't known at the time, but the woman had contracted The Virus. She had been taken to The Bubble: an extensive facility created to isolate infected individuals. The thought of The Bubble had become one of Mable's greatest fears, and she couldn't bear the thought of anyone she loved being taken away.

But standing on their beach, The Bubble seemed like some fictional place generated to keep her safe in this village. Eventually, she guided Jupiter home after staring out into the dwindling light for a while, his tear-stained face blotchy, his eyes weary. His expression held the same desperation that it had some seven years ago, when they had first met, back when he would cry for hours on end, and no amount of comforting seemed to settle him. Mable felt like the same confused little girl she had been, unable to find the right words to make all of her new brother's tears subside.

As soon as the door closed behind them, their dad appeared in the hallway with a warm smile and rosy cheeks. Jupiter ran past him, head bowed, straight up the stairs. They heard a door slam from above. Josh turned to Mable with a raised brow. "What's wrong with him?"

"He's upset again. He wants to leave this place – he knows he can't, but he was born to explore. You know what he's like." She chuckled bitterly, unable to look at her dad as she fumbled with Margot's lead. "He'll be fine. I just wish he didn't feel like this, and I wish it was all different, and-"

A hand on her shoulder broke her voice, and she drew an unsteady breath. "Honey, we can get caught up on all the wishes we have. But in the end, we just have to make do with what we've been given."

"But what if it's not enough for him?" If her dad had an answer, he didn't say it. Instead, he held her to his chest fiercely.

They climbed the stairs together after that, and Mable left her dad knocking softly on Jupiter's bedroom door. On entering her room, she saw the familiar knitted jumper of Emmi's. The soft material brought a gentle smile to her face despite a growing weight in her stomach for her brother. She smoothed out its creases, then stopped abruptly as something bright red caught her eye. The bright colour disappeared from sight as she laid the sweater out on the bed. Mable held her breath, and peeled back the neat fold of the jumper.

There was an odd, glowing, deep-red light, no bigger than a grain of rice. Perplexed at the sight, she blinked as if to erase it from her vision. With no success, Mable brought the jumper closer to her face. It didn't look familiar, not lint that she could remove easily. It looked almost as if it was part of the material itself, glistening and intertwined in the fabric. Unwilling to touch the unknown, Mable set down the jumper on the bed and reached into her pocket for her phone. She would text Emmi a photo to clarify, she felt like it was an overreaction, but she'd experienced enough abnormality for one day. Focusing the camera to the red below, Mable noticed the lack of replica in the image on the screen. With shallow breaths, she wiped the screen clutched in her hands. No red appeared.

A rush of realisation hit her and, gasping, she let the jumper escape her grasp, watching it as it fell to the ground.

Lead in her stomach, ice in her veins, her panic fuelled mind drove her to step back away from the jumper, on impulse, as if it were some sort of vicious creature. But her logical mind soon took over. She had to wash The Virus off before it multiplied, spread and wreaked havoc. Mable grabbed the jumper, careful not to touch the red mark, and rushed to the bathroom, locking the door firmly behind her. In an attempt to extinguish the tiny speck that had the potential to destroy so much, she threw it into the sink, snatched a bar of soap and began to scrub furiously.

Mind racing, her hands moved with more and more fervour, desperation hanging in every movement. Coils wrapped around her chest, constricting her breathing into frantic gulps, and she grit her teeth against the onslaught of terror threatening to drown her. The water, still flowing in ever blistering temperatures, beganto scald Mable's hands as her eyes blurred with all-encompassing fear. This couldn't be happening. She was sure it would never happen, not to her, not to Emmi, not to Jupiter. She continued to scrub to avoid thinking about all the possible repercussions this could have for her and for her brother. If she could just erase this seemingly insignificant spore, everything would be okay. Tears burned in her eyes as she rinsed off the lather and drew in a shuddering breath in anticipation. Scanning the pool of murky green for signs of the offending red, she found it had vanished. A sigh escaped her as she dragged the sodden fabric from the basin, squeezing the excess water into the shadowy depths below.

After pressing an ear to the bathroom door to check if the landing was deserted, she hastily glided across the hall and slid into her bedroom, softly shutting the door behind her. Mable tucked the damp green bundleonto the radiator to dry, now she was sure it was decontaminated. The adrenaline, now deserting her, left her trembling uncontrollably, drained and alert all at once. Lethargic and depleted, Mable fell back against her bed. But despite her trembling hands, she finally took a breath, letting the relief fill her chest. It was gone.Shuffling herself up the bed and burying her face in her pillow, she eventually fell into a fitful sleep.

Red. Alarm bells in colour, a warning painting the walls in its ominous swathes. Clusters of minute, fiery pinpricks scattered across the room like crimson constellations, paralysing Mable with fear as her eyesdarted around the room as if to find an escape. Trying to take a deep breath and failing only led to further panic. Her whole body had been drained of warmth. Her jaw chattered, her muscles tensed, her hands were ice cold. Mable pressed the heel of her hand to her eyes, sucking in sharp painful breaths as she willed herself to stay in control.

The rush of blood in her ears was constant and far from calming as her racing heart made her chest heave. Filled with an unexplainable energy, Mable jumped up on shaky legs and stood in the centre of her room, surrounded by a sea of scarlet. The four walls spun around her, taunting her vulnerability and helplessness. She imagined this was how the woman had felt when she was taken away in the black van – she couldn't help but think whether she or her brother would be sentenced to the same fate. Jupiter. This was her fault. If only she hadn't got this chip. But it wouldn't be different, only that she wouldn't have the ability to see it.

If Jupiter caught it…

Unable to pick out a single thought from the hurricane of fear, which looped between wanting to run and feeling rooted to the floor, she peered around the room with a scream stuck in her throat. She didn't even know who or what she'd be calling for. Part of her thought she could call for her dad and it would all go away, but she knew it was impossible. He couldn't save her anymore, couldn't be her hero and wipe away her tears, because this was something more than just a scraped knee. Who could stop this?

Hands shaking, she clutched them together and glanced down to see the same crimson particles tarnishing her fingers. Another surge of panic washed over her with such intensity that she almost lost her balance. Mechanically pushing her hands away, Mable began to scratch at her skin, her craving to purge herself of it made her oblivious to any pain. Desperation built inside her she scratched harder and with less and less restraint, her hands erratically working of their own accord, driven by raw utter panic. Tears blinded her, shocks of fiery discomfort only gave her further determination, despite her hands growing slick with blood and sweat. Her eyes darted around her room for some means of cleansing and fell upon a bottle of sanitiser. She scrambled for it. Frantically, she shook the last of the bottle onto her palm and bit her tongue to suppress a shriek of agony. Stomach twisting, she rubbed it into her wounded hands despite the burning, watching as the glowing spores disappeared, replaced by darker stains of blood. Frantically trying to turn away from the encroaching walls surrounding her, Mable studied the room, hoping some other decontaminator would reveal itself so she could be free of this nightmare. Instead, she found herself gazing, transfixed, towards her mirror.

Cautiously, she stepped towards it and looked through the glass to see another place. The blemishes of red that were burned into her mind were absent, as if the mirror were a time-capsule. Except her hands still bore the wounds of her repulsion, and the anxiety that stemmed from The Virus. The room beyond the glass was waking up to rays of morning sunshine, and jovial bird song that filled the space with a graceful, taunting tranquillity. Only marred by the handprint of glistening ruby left by the girl in the mirror.

Abby Mayers and Melody Lumb are A-Level students and aspiring writers from Cheshire. In their rare free time, they can usually be found together, exploring both fictional universes and the natural world. Due to Covid restrictions, they had to work on Crimson Constellations outdoors, competing with the Autumn weather and ever shortening days. The evolution of their short story was impacted by the constant shifting of a society in the midst of a global pandemic. They had never written together prior to their hearing of the Teens of Tomorrow competition, but discovered that they instantly found a rhythm to writing as a pair, encouraging and challenging each other to delve into their imaginations to discover their futuristic, dystopian society dictated by 'The Virus'. Both Abby and Melody are eager to see where writing will take them in the future, and are already considering revisiting characters from Crimson Constellations and developing their stories, as well as creating new worlds and people. One of the uniting forces between Abby and Melody's relationship as co-authors is their shared desire to represent both the unique and diverse society that the modern day facilitates and the individual complexity of empathy, alongside understanding of finger-print emotion in every situation, projected through this world and the characters residing within them.

Swamp Reeds

Mary Ball Howkins

I am the oldest girl at sixteen, and I am supposed to know what to do when no adult is here. Mamma goes with the other women to the next village to sell and trade vegetables, and Papa is away working in a gold mine, always away. He works underground at the bottom of a wide, yellow hole in the ground, filling a small truck on wheels. He comes home on two buses for a short stay after many weeks.

Our thatched huts are empty today. Village men took firewood by wagon to prepare the neighboring school for cooler months. The only sounds are made by chickens pecking at the ground: those funny watery sounds, gossiping among themselves. They wander in and out of the rows of upright sticks which guard our circle of eight round shelters. They face inward, toward each other for protection. I am still thin enough to squeeze between the posts. My legs are like poles, but I'm lucky only my legs need go through the short posts, and not my butt.

My sister, Lindiwe, is not much more than a baby. She has perfect teeth, better than mine, long legs and arms, and a shy smile. Yet her dancing eyes show the inner gaiety that delights all in our village. And her body hides a baby.

Her stomach is small, so we did not suspect anything, and neither did she. Lindiwe is too young to know this about herself. We knew nothing until the waters flowed out of her after Mamma left. That made me remember Mamma's waters and thank the goddess Mamlambo for her river signal.

I tried not to feel panic when the water came. I pushed the knot in my throat down toward my knees. Looking around our village for help, I saw no one, not one man hoeing in the field, a man who could run to market for Mamma or our birther Auntie. I called out, hoping for just one person, but no one came to any hut door. The rounded openings were dark and empty. I have tried to push the feelings back, but now my knees shake.

How can I do this?

There is only my brother, Kagiso, and me to bring this baby to earth. My brother weeds behind our house. His muscles are strong for a boy of twelve, and he was born with all the beauty the ancestors could muster. His brown-nut, solid body shines with sweat in the sun. He works hard for us at raising what we eat, and already made a fence of reeds around our garden. Mamma made him do it so the smaller animals cannot easily get to our food. Birds can, and that is a problem, so we have hung pieces of plastic and metal from a string over the plants. Sometimes when the sun is sharp, these work, but sometimes they don't. Birds are smart and wait for shadow. My little brother has not yet outsmarted them.

Is he enough of a man to be of use for this baby?

Reed work must be done with care. The care is to thank our traditional god, Unkulunkulu, the creator of all. His name means "the greatest one." He was made in Uhlanga, a big swamp of reeds, before he came to earth. Unkulunkulu taught my people the skills of hunting and planting. He was a reed who took a human form, so we Zulu honor reeds. Our king sometimes hosts a reed dance for young maidens. Each young woman brings the King a reed as a sign of her maidenhood.

Lindiwe is not a maiden. There is a child in her belly. Am I wise enough to bring that child into this life, just me?

When I ask her whose baby she has, her face makes a smiling beauty, but she is silent. She will not tell, and perhaps she does not even know. She is more than innocent. Mamma says she is simple:

that her body grows, yet her mind stays a child. Most of the time she is happy, the happiest of all of us. Brilliant colored insects make her happy, even small glowing rocks. She has made a collection of these insects and talks to every one of them like a friend. Our home has many praying mantises where she sleeps on her mat, and Lindiwe says they talk to her. At night, Mamma makes her put them in a grass cage, so we don't crush them as we dream. Lindiwe weeps, almost without stopping, when she finds a dead one in many pieces.

Some women at the trading village where Mamma walks say that Lindiwe's simpleness is a curse from our ancestors. I wonder whose ancestors. Mamma's? Papa's? Did someone anger them? We should know this tale of anger, but we don't, so how can it be true? The Christian lady who came said nature made Lindiwe this way. For us, our gods give us nature, all the good things that come from plants, the sun and water. Unkulunkulu is our first ancestor. He gave us my sister for some reason. Did we anger him, or another god? Did Mamma? Did I?

I will need Kagiso's help in birthing this baby. My stomach rolls up into my throat. There is no one but Kagiso. He is four years younger than me, and often silly. I hope he will be serious when the time comes. I remember when he was born: an auntie came from a close village to help him and Mamma along. Papa wasn't there to see his boy push out.

Mamma's birth times are long. Mine was long. She always says "too long", and that she was worn out by the end, and stayed on her mat with me for two days. She tells me that I liked it, that time after my birth. I was calm and slept a lot, always beside her while she rested. A golden bird flew in the open door, a good omen for me and for my father, she believed. She knew then South Africa would never run out of gold, and Papa could keep his job. She worries about his job often, because some miners were killed when they complained about their pay. She made him promise not to complain. When she wasn't listening, I made him promise too, the last time he was here.

How can I help my sister? Maybe the birth will be so long that the women will arrive back from market to take over. What do I remember about my brother's birth? I was only three, but Mamma and I slept together in the one bed in our only room. I was there, closely watching. No one shooed me out. They were too busy, Mamma and the auntie. A few chickens wandered in and out, but that was all. I thought a bad spirit was killing Mamma when she cried out in pain. But when Kagiso came out upside down, I knew it must be a good spirit who brought babies. But upside down? And why this spirit brought them through such a difficult door was a mystery.

Lindiwe came when I was four. I remember more about *her* birth. Mamma had already taught me a little about Kagiso's, so I was more prepared. Never prepared for Mamma's screaming though, or the blood that came with her. Or the slap awake when my sister pushed out. Mamma said I could help clean Lindiwe, so I did. I used a cloth dipped in warm water and gently wiped away the goo all over her tiny body. We made a good team, the auntie and me. Two tender baby cleaners. We wrapped her in a new cloth, a special small one, mostly yellow and blue.

Now that I am to be in charge, panic rises again and my legs wobble. I look around into the grasses and trees to find plants that can help. When the soap bush catches my attention, my shaking eases, but my knees still feel weak. It's the perfect plant, with large pliable leaves for wrapping a baby, and stopping blood flow if I need them. My heart skips and a giant breath rises from my toes to my head, bringing some calm. Nature can help the three of us do this together.

"How are you feeling now?" I ask my sister, who is slumped in shade against the outdoor wall of our home.

"Sick, after the waters left." She speaks in a raspy voice. "There is strange movement inside me, like I ate something not good." She pats her tummy, and then slowly sits up straight like a tree trunk, her eyes widening. "Ohhhhhhh." Sound rushes from her mouth. "Aiiiiiiiiii."

I call in my loudest voice. "Kagiso, come! It is time!"

He comes fast from the garden with his hands covered in dirt. His eyes are wider than ours when he sees Lindiwe sliding up against the wall, moving to stand upright with her mouth drawn long in a silent scream.

"Wash your hands with only the clean water, not what's left from cooking," I say. "Go to the soap bush for a good medicine clean, then rinse well." He runs fast, so I know he is frightened. He is young and scared of seeing a baby born. It will make him less of a man someday, he said that over and over when we talked in the morning. "Only women help with a birth," he had whined. "My duty is to pray." This he said with his face scrunched up like a monkey.

"You will have to do more than pray today, or this baby may die," I told him. "And besides, you will be a smarter man knowing how god decided to have babies come to earth."

Perhaps my words are still on his mind, at least it keeps any more whines from leaving his mouth as he rushes to where the soap bushes grow in a family group.

I help Lindiwe inside to Mamma's mat. To me it is the birthing mat, washed many times in its life. Three times after babies. I try to help her lie down, but she fights me.

"I will do this on my legs." She speaks in a weak voice, full of breath.

She looks into my eyes with fierceness and lets her body slowly move into to a squat next to the side wall. Her left arm braces her on the piece of wood that follows the ground's direction, and I hold her elbow on the right. We stay like that while she breathes deeply, strengthening the balance of her body. I am afraid to let go, but she knocks my arm loose with an elbow shake. She lets her legs and the thick weave of the wall be her support.

"Where did you see this?" I ask.

"When the auntie helped a woman in a field. She said to the woman it could be faster if the baby just dropped." Lindiwe gives me a shallow smile. "You see," she says, "I am smarter than Mamma thinks."

"You *are*. And you are much smarter than I am, sister. You drop, and we will catch the little one." I stand close and make a catching motion under her. Her mouth makes a tiny curve. "I hope I remember how to get you there. I was small when you were born, but a birth stays in memory. It is noisy and messy each time. When he finishes washing, I will tell our brother to help prepare us. And don't worry, I have washed too."

"I have no worries about your hands, only how to get this baby out of me," she replies in a scratchy voice.

I have those same worries. Maybe Mamma will come back early. It will take her two hours to walk to the village market and two hours back. She carried a full basket on her head. I hope she sells fast. Kagiso stops in a burst of dust at the door, his panicked look reminding me that I am in charge. I straighten to ease what we must be doing.

"Get a clean cloth." I say to my brother.

His eyes blink as he leans in the doorway. "What is she doing?"

"She is getting herself in a good position to drop the baby. Quick. Get a cloth." He races to our few clean cloths, each rolled up separately in a jug. I hope they will be enough, but then I remember the pliable leaves outside. The cloth he chooses is a dark red, with thin stripes of blue. It will do well to hide the blood that babies bring.

The baby does not come quickly. It wishes to be slow to join us, despite Lindiwe's position. Maybe we are in too big of a hurry for it. It is small, and maybe scared of leaving its mother. We wait long and think Mamma will return to be in charge. I put a stool under my sister to ease her legs. Waiting is hard. Kagiso and I let our sister's praying mantises climb up and down our hands. We feed them ants and other insects to keep them happy and walking back to us. Their bodies can break easily, so we are careful to treat them well. This makes Lindiwe smile. They are her babies too.

The wait is long and hot, until shadows creep through the doorway. The sun goes past the eagle's spot in the sky, looking for the mopane trees. We are grateful for the sun's path of leaving. If only it would bring the women back from market. Lindiwe's breathing is rapid now, so I tell her to push, the way Mamma did for her. Pushing is not usual for my sister, but after a few minutes she does it better and better. Her face collapses like an over ripe pumpkin. She cries out with each push. I wait. When will a head come to welcome and support?

I am frightened that the pushing will be long, and Lindiwe will become too exhausted to stay on her feet as she plans. "Let the base of your back settle more into the wall," I tell her as she leaves the stool behind. "We can't let your legs give way too soon. The center pole that balances the tall ones can be a support." She lowers her body an inch to brace her hips and slowly smiles with her lips parted.

In minutes she pushes again with more conviction. A deep pelvic shove brings enough sweat to completely flatten the small bit of hair she has. "That was *the* push," I murmur. "A head?" I ask out loud of myself. "Yes," I say to Lindiwe, with a rush of air to match hers. "Kagiso, the cloth." He stands close with his cloth, eyes wide with fear.

"Push. Push, sister…Push harder," I yell. She pushes deeply, urgently, to meet her child, and cries out like a hawk sighting prey.

"Shoulders! I see shoulders," Kagiso calls, his voice so loud it grates my ears.

My brother does the right thing without me saying a word. He drops to his knees and holds his cloth to catch Lindiwe's falling baby. It comes fast after the shoulders break free.

A boy. It's a boy. Its cry is loud as Kagiso folds the blue and red cloth over its tiny body and uses a clean knife to cut its mother-cord. We dip small cloths into a bowl of water, warmed by the sun, to clean the baby's face and hair. Precious black hair, like the fuzz outside a fallen nut. The baby quiets to our soft touch. Kagiso holds him like Lindiwe cradles a mantis.

My sister, the mother of this baby. I have forgotten her. Lindiwe leans against the wall, her face and hair sparkling with sweat, her eyes full of fighting emotions: terror and love. The baby's soft blanket from inside her is at her feet. She made no sound when it came out. I look to Kagiso and the newborn.

"Hand him to your sister," I whisper, giving Lindiwe back her stool. She sits to hold her son, my baby sister with a dear one all her own. I come to her side to see him. "This is a baby like your mantises, just as precious, wholly human. You must care for him as you do for them, Lindiwe. He is as delicate as their small green bodies. He must sleep safely beside you and come to no harm."

A tight smile captures her lips, yet when a mantis lands on her baby's cloth, it loosens to a full curve on her face. Her lips release a small laugh into the air, and then they kiss her baby's forehead. She is too young, but she will love this child. As will I. We will both be its mother, as I have been Lindiwe's, along with Mamma.

What will our Mamma say when she returns with the sun's long shadows? What will our kin and neighbors think of this child and what man's it is? Will they welcome it in Nature's own way, or believe it a curse from our ancestors? Will they hunt for the father by talking among themselves, probing its time of conception, or questioning and alarming Lindiwe?

What will Papa say? Another mouth to feed? No. I hope, a gift from the reed god, Unkulunkulu. Our God has brought us a child, a reed in his own shape, brought to earth on Mamma's thin cane mat. I will tell our kin and neighbors our family is *blessed* with a second boy.

Mary Ball Howkins writes for and about southern African youth. Her stories reveal some of the challenges young Africans face and the successes they achieve against difficult odds, human and animal. Her experiences as an African wildlife, school and orphanage volunteer have informed the narratives she weaves.

The Zebra Genus

A. Rose

Outside the doors, the world is always changing.

Where to start? I guess the world is as good a place as any to begin. The world is so full. Full of people, 8 billion of us, who are all full of dreams. It's bursting with countries and cultures, and a million different pathways. Like the millions of neural pathways that exist inside our brains, that allow us to have these thoughts and dreams and worlds inside our heads. We could live a thousand lives to completion and still never get to experience it all. Which makes me excited for where my next life might take me. As for the current me, I plan to experience as much of it as I can before I go. Whether it's France, or Spain, or that beautiful road we drove down between

Italy and Austria, we are lucky to be where we are now. Now, in this very moment, we are infinite.

Even though we have been parked up in the same place for a couple of weeks, it's a different view every time I look out. As the salty sea air erodes the cliff's edge, so do the waves below, moulding and shaping the stone to their will. It's formidable, this cliff, but not formidable enough.

I take the pencil out of my mouth, suddenly aware of the teeth marks I have gnawed into its end, whilst my thoughts were away somewhere out there. No wonder my jaw is aching.

My name is Penelope. Or Nell. Or Pen. Depends who you talk to.

I pause, not really sure what you're supposed to include in these things. When everything that happens in your life is so serious, it's hard to write anything serious about it. I rotate my hand feeling the tendons grind together beneath my skin, causing a wince from the bruise I didn't notice I had until now.

I'm seventeen. And I'm a Zebra. You may ask how I came to this conclusion. You see, doctors are taught to assess a patient's symptoms, and look for the most obvious and likely cause. 'When you hear hoof beats, think horse, not zebra'. So whilst they looked for all of the obvious reasons for my symptoms: the subluxation of my shoulders, and the hypermobility of my fingers, I went through a

whole bunch of different pills and physio to help try to manage the
pain. I suppose it doesn't help that I bruise really easy, so with that,
and the dislocations, I think people thought I was being beaten for a
while. A notion which did not sit well with my parents, I'll tell you
that. It took them a long time to realise that I'm not a horse after all,
because I have Vascular Ehlers Danlos Syndrome.

The side door of the van slides open, and I resist the urge to throw the notebook and pencil under the blanket wrapped around me. Gemma would definitely know that something's up. Instead, I close the pages of the book slowly, and smile at her as she shrugs off her coat and dumps her boots at the door. Then she notices me looking at her.

"You okay?" She asks in that nonchalant way that smooths over all the concern at the edges of her tone.

"Yeah" I lie with a small shrug.

She would hate it if she knew I was writing a Eulogy. Not because I'm dying or anything. Just because I might. Die. Some time.

I came pretty close last year and… well I guess it's good to be prepared. Just in case. I like the idea of someone reading my words at my funeral, as if, even posthumously, I have to have the final say. Gem is busy pouring miscellaneous items out of her backpack. She puts the food she has just bought into the kitchen cupboards, and the butter in the fridge. She's muttering away to herself, complaining that the supermarket never has all of the things we need, and 'If you're gonna shop half-arsed, why bother shopping at all'.

"Leave the butter out?" I ask.

She turns, painfully slowly to look at me, one eyebrow raised, jaw locked. This is a 'discussion' we have all the time.

"It belongs in the fridge."

"If you put it in there it'll go hard and then it's too difficult to spread."

"You're not the one who spreads it. My spreading skills, my rules."

I can't help but smirk a little at that.

"We don't want a repeat of last time" She persists.

I left the butter out on the shelf, and it melted on a hot day. Admittedly, it was unfortunately placed, right above the toaster. The poor thing was spitting out black tar for weeks afterwards, kind of like my blood vessels- a grim reminder to us both. I bow my head, gracefully conceding to her point. This time. She snorts and shuts the fridge.

Outside the doors, the world is changing again. It's getting close to sunset, and there's this beautiful red sky that's making its way down to meet the ocean below it.

There used to be so much space in this van, back when I had

the strength to tuck the Murphy bed up into the wall. Somewhere underneath here is a sofa, but it's been so long since we've seen it that I can't even remember the colour of the fabric. It's been a particularly bad flare this time, all that hiking and swimming and good food was always going to catch up with me, but these last few weeks in bed have set my bones back in place, and I'm finally on the mend. Sure, there are bruises and aches, the odd twinge and twist in the wrong direction, but those are a kind of liveable pain.

It was Gemma's idea to buy the van. An entire lecture had come with it, about how the price of a house nowadays is ridiculously unachievable, and how we'd be setting ourselves up for a failure if we tied ourselves down to one of those stuffy Victorian builds. And I mean, there's definitely truth to that. For the price of a deposit, or the down payment on a mortgage, we managed to get ourselves a 1986 Toyota Hiace, in which we shoved our double mattress, propped up a makeshift kitchen, and a little pipe with running water as a sorry excuse for a bathroom. But really, she did it for me. She'd never admit it, but the reason she spent all her savings on this old rust bucket we live in, is so that I would get to see the world like I always wanted. So I traded in my two wheels for four, and we set off as soon as the hospital said I was well enough.

There's this Chinese proverb-legend thing, that talks about a fine red string tied to the end of each person's little finger. And the other end is tied to the finger of the person you are meant to be with. I guess it depends if you believe in 'meant to be' and all that. Sometimes your red thread might get wrapped around the wrong person, or tangled up in all sorts of different directions, but it will always lead you to the person your ribbon is tied to eventually. I believe in 'meant to be'. And seeing as Gemma has the other end of my string, I'll follow wherever she goes.

A big part of our ribbon is wrapped around my disability, and it comes with a lot of little knots in it. One for worrying (I'm world class at that) about all of the things I haven't got around to doing yet, and find myself too tired to complete. One for guilt, for relying on her to take care of me sometimes, when the EDS flares and I'm too unwell to wash or dress, or even talk much. One for mum and dad, who are grateful to Gem for helping me really see the world, rather than watch it go by without me, but who are also scared of missing out on these days with me. But the two most important knots are the ones right at each end. They're tied so tight they won't ever come loose.

"Nell...?"

Gem echoes somewhere beyond the words of my letter.

"Hello? Nell."

"Huh? What?" I snap back into focus.

"Do you want me to shut the back doors?" Gem offers,

bringing me out of my head like she always does. I knew there was a reason I keep her around.

I shake my head and drag the duvet up around my chest, hunkering down into the bed to stave off the chill that is slowly creeping in.

"It's so nice to have them open, I love watching the waves break."

It's the only thing I can think of that feels more wild and powerful the more it breaks.

"Nell?"

I turn to see Gemma holding out a mug of hot chocolate, and the smell of pumpkin spice drifts across the van to meet me. She grins.

"I swear I spend half of my life with my hand outstretched, waiting for you to take something I'm offering."

I lean over and take the two mugs from her as she climbs up into the bed. It suddenly feels massive as she crawls across it towards me, overcoming the mountain of blankets and pillows between us.

She tucks her legs in beside me and snuggles in close, looking past me to the empty horizon. It doesn't take her long to return to her familiar habit of absent-mindedly tracing the blue veins across my arms with her fingertip. Her hands are cold. The condition makes my skin a lot thinner than normal, so the web of veins underneath are almost see-through. They look like the venation patterns you see when you hold a leaf up to the sunlight. And just like a leaf, my skin tears easily, as do the veins underneath. My organs too. That's how I ended up in the hospital last year.

I pick up the notebook, tilting it slightly so that Gemma can't see the words I am writing. She's too distracted by the things that exist beyond us to notice anyway.

Pain is normal for me, that's another lucky symptom of EDS, but late last fall I woke up in the night to an out-of-the-ordinary kind of agony. It started off as though a tiny flower had bloomed across my abdomen, but as Gem lifted my shirt up, the flower spread further and further around my side, like someone had walked across the skin there and left bruises where they had trodden. The rest of the night was a blur of words like 'perforated' and 'haemorrhaged', which eventually came down to internal bleeding, and a month-long residency in the recovery unit.

I catch Gemma's fingers and lift them up to my lips, kissing them softly. She's looking at my face now, but I get the sense that she is seeing more than just that. I am conscious of the red thread pulling on my finger. There's this kind of feeling that I get when I look at her. Like it doesn't matter about the ridiculous price of housing, or the world outside us disappearing so fast it might not be here one day. And I might not be either. Somehow, looking at her

150

makes all of that ok.

"I've been writing something."

She smiles. "Read it to me."

"It's for you, for when I'm gone." Before I can stop them, the words are out.

"Pen..." she warns. That's the name she likes to use when she is cross with me.

She knows it's been on my mind a lot lately, there's only so long we can keep dancing around it. But she must know this time that I'm serious, because suddenly her face softens.

"I suppose I had better read it then. Your spelling is awful."

I laugh and wince: even the small things are hard when your ribs are made of glass. Gemma squeezes my hand softly, not mentioning my obvious discomfort, and she begins to read what I have written. Her dark eyes absorb my words, but her face remains still, showing no sign of what is running through her head.

I look back to the vastness outside the van, where the light has all but diminished, and the tide draws the waves back into the salty belly of the sea. It's settling down a bit, no more waves crash down against the beach, or chip away slowly at the cliffs. The fragility of these waves is clearer now, in these last moments of daylight. They are born, grow, and die, again and again, just like the 8 billion of us. Just like the neural pathways of our brains. Our thoughts. Our dreams. The worlds inside our heads. We spend our lives trying to make our mark on this earth in the short time we have, like the marks those waves have left on the landscape.

Looking at Gemma, I know that she is my mark in this lifetime. Her soul is the cliff just outside, a strong, sturdy, beautiful soul, that has been changed and shaped around my own, eroded over time by my waves. I know how hard it will be for her to watch me crash when the time comes, and none of us ever really know how long that will be. But for now, our sea is as endless as the horizon, with all the days and weeks and years stretching before it.

As she finishes reading, her dark eyes rise to meet mine.

"Will you walk with me?" I whisper. "The world outside is changing, and it's time I get out of this bed and see some more of it."

A. Rose is a Creative Writing Graduate from UEA. Her work focuses on reframing disability, as well as the psychology of memories. She recently won first place in the Science me a Story 2019 competition, with her piece 'The Nodes of Ranvier'. She is fascinated by myths and legends and loves writing about nature. She travels the world in a self-converted van with her fiancé and their Bedlington Whippet.

Find her at: www.write-a-rose.com

Pax Park

Margaret Forze

"Hi, thank you for choosing Bluefield Jane's, what can I get-"

A loud voice booms through the headset, cutting off my line. "UM YEAH I WANT A DOUBLE CHEESEBURGER WITH EVERYTHING ON IT EXCEPT FOR ONION – NO ONION – AND I WANT FRIES AND A CHOCOLATE SHAKE WITH THAT. ALSO I AM A SENIOR SO I WANT THE SENIOR DISCOUNT."

My little fingers scramble to keep up with his demands, desperately searching the computer screen for the right buttons to press. "I'm sorry, you said no onion on that?"

"YES, NO ONION...*idiot*," he mutters to himself. I take a deep breath. "Alrighty then, anything else I can get for you today?"

"DID YOU GET MY SENIOR DISCOUNT? I DON'T SEE IT"

In... and out... "Yes, I got it."

"Good," he states, before letting the engine roar and quite possibly damaging my hearing for the foreseeable future. I sigh as he pulls up to the window, taking yet another deep breath and regaining my composure as the car rolls forward. Everyday I deal with this crap, and yet I never fail to dig my fingernails so deep into my palms little crescents form. All I can do at this point is hope that my happy place will calm me. *Close my eyes, count to three, let this peace stay with me.*

"Your total is going to be $8.38," I say with an extremely fake smile (not that he would know the difference) as I pull open the window.

The man slowly puts his car into park, then begins the painstakingly long process of counting out 38 cents in what appears to be mostly pennies. I start to look around the restaurant to keep my sanity and realize that there is now a line of cars waiting to be helped. Fantastic.

After what seems like a decade, he shoves the change towards me, my pinky just barely saving a runaway nickel. I plug the cash into the register, then hand out his shake, but not before seriously considering giving him a small taste of my tainted Gen-Z DNA. I stick the number of his order on his car.

"Sir if you could go ahead and pull forward..." he steps on the gas mid-sentence. I feel my shoulders drop as I tiredly close the window, losing all my energy looking at the monitor and seeing a pile-up of cars. *Minimum wage is not nearly enough for this shit.* I breathe out, square my shoulders, then click the ON button on my microphone. "Hi, thank you for choosing Bluefield Jane's, what can I get for you today?"

I've worked at Jane's for just around two years now. Being an ex-convict doesn't look too good on job resumes, but I got lucky with Jane's. Well, I guess that depends on your definition of 'lucky'.

"Hi yes, I need a kids tender meal with chocolate milk and a plain cheeseburger."

I needed a job to pay the bills. I'm only 18 years old; my parents kicked me out at 17 because of my sexuality, and things went to shit pretty soon after that. I still graduated with my high school degree, but I ran into a bit of trouble with the law...

"Are fries okay with that?"

"Yes that's fine."

Luckily, the judge took it pretty easy on me. Only 40 hours of community service and the charges were dropped. He said it was because I seemed like a good kid who had just lost her way, but I'm pretty sure it was less about my moral values and more about the fact that I'm white, Christian, and the daughter of two small town church celebrities. Wonder what he would have said if he had known I was gay.

"Is that gonna be all for you today?"

"Yes it is."

"Your total is going to be $9.53 at the window."

After I finished my hours I worked to get my life back on track. I crashed with a couple of friends until I was able to afford my own place, and now here I am, working at a fast food chain to bring in rent and some sort of hope for a college education.

An older woman in her forties rolls up to the window, her arm already extended, handing me her card as she hushes a toddler sitting in the back. I hand her a chocolate milk. "If you can go ahead and pull forward we'll be out with you shortly." She nods with a friendly smile as she leaves the window spot vacant, waiting to be filled by the next customer.

Don't get me wrong, not all the customers are terrible. We actually have several people who gush smiles, energy, and positivity.

Like the one old man who tells me a new dad joke every time he comes through, or the teen who makes sure to tell me how good of a job I'm doing no matter how long she has to wait. Unfortunately, there are also a lot of assholes, who tend to dim the bright lights in my often dark days. And then I am lost and alone, scared of what comes searching for me next, completely susceptible to falling victim to any sort of life, no matter how evil.

Outside of work, it's a mixture of good and bad, clawing at each other's throats. They compete for the spotlight, not realizing that in doing so, their purpose is lost on me. But I listen anyway – I mean, what am I supposed to do? The commotion keeps me sane. At least it's better than the commotion in my head. Social media promotes the 'good'" and 'bad'. Instagram, Tik Tok, Snapchat, Twitter, Facebook; it's all the same. The hearts go up, and the awareness does as well. Copy link then share –it's a routine at this point. Over and over and over again, crying laughing, crying sadness, crying anger. There's love and there's hate- but one thing is for sure, there's nothing but knowing.

Especially now, everyone and everywhere are opening their mouths, speaking, talking, discussing, yelling, screaming. These people —my people— these kids and young adults, are speaking out. They take the monsters in their mind, the struggles of their souls, and channel them into words. A remixed dictionary in our generation, they speak feelings of passion and importance, even if they don't speak at all. They are a collective voice, needing to be heard, waiting to be heard. They are change. Not everything they say has the most positive tone, or even the friendliest. In fact, things are pretty bad. There's a lot of hate in this world, and it seems to get worse every day. But at least they're saying it.

A little gray Toyota pulls up past my window as I think to myself, flashing a bright bumper sticker with the words, STOP GLOBAL WARMING AND SAVE THE POLAR BEARS accompanying a little cartoon polar bear. My next customer has a tattoo on her arm that pokes out as she reaches forward, reading HER STORY as a picture of the "We Can Do It!" lady dangles from the rearview mirror of her blue Jeep Wrangler. I can feel my inner passions getting fired up just looking at it, thinking of all the many reasons this lady's stance was one of truth and equality. *Maybe I should tell her…*

"Sophrona!" My lazy boss's raspy, hollering voice breaks my train of thought, "We're out of cups up here!"

I wave the lady forward, and reluctantly turn towards the storage room.

"Coming!"

Other than getting sucked into all the drama in the world, there is one other constant in my life. That place is Pax Park. This beautiful metropark a couple miles from home, it stretches for miles, a town in that of itself. Oh, and what a town it is! Hundreds of people, every day, coming from all around just to soak in the sun, walk with old friends, swim with the kayakers or run with the bikers. And in the middle of it all is this gorgeous lake, stretching so long it seems as though there's no end. That body of water is the epicenter of what I call my last chance at peace in this life.

Pax is sort of a savior to me. A while back, I realized that I was seriously losing my will to live. I would wake up and immediately wish that I hadn't, desperately trying to bring back the neutral world in which I wasn't dead, but I sure as hell wasn't living this nightmare. Sometimes it worked, sometimes it didn't. But either way, at some point, I would have to rise. That was the hardest part of my day, and it was slowly shifting into a task that was surely unbearable.

I started searching for meaning, or something to give me happiness, no matter how small. For example, I tried painting the sunrise. That resulted in such intense crabbiness and frustration I punched a hole in the canvas and sent the paint brush flying into the downstairs neighbor's shrubbery. It made for an interesting conversation starter with the testosterone filled male who lives there, but I think his focus was on something that I, as a female who is attracted to people with mainly estrogen, could not provide him.

I also dabbled in the art of cooking, but after an egg yolk ended up on the ceiling, I decided that that may not be the one for me either. From there it was an entire lifetime of hobbies. I tried running, dancing, gardening, photography, reading, writing, drawing, knitting and even singing, which ended up being at the mercy of my neighbors, who would much rather listen to the birds in comparison to my screeching.

Then, one morning, a coworker asked me if I wanted to go biking with her at Pax. Seeing as it was only a couple minutes from my apartment and she had generously offered me an old bike of hers, I agreed with much enthusiasm. After that, I was hooked. For the rest of that day I spent every waking moment thinking about riding. I couldn't get over how wonderful it felt; the wind on my tired face, my feet circling around and around, the adrenaline pumping through my legs as I conquered that one big hill around the corner. It was freeing to know that for once in my life, I was the one in control.

From that day on, I have biked that trail every single day. An eight mile loop around the lake, it began to feel like it had managed to embed itself into my veins, becoming a huge part of who I am. Over time, my coworker called it quits, claiming that she had grown tired and lazy and much too devoid of the energy I had so much of. Luckily, she offered me her old bike, letting me hang on to it for good. Once my coworker was gone, the loop turned into 16 miles, then 24, and then even 32 on the best of days. I found myself setting an alarm just to get up in the mornings and fit in even more mileage than I had the day before. Work no longer seemed like a drag, all because I knew that working meant that I was getting through the day, and getting through the day meant that I was reaching the night, which would end and bring the beginning of yet another bike ride at sunrise, which looked much better when it wasn't in pastel.

For a solid couple of months, that was my life. I would awake to bike, then deal with the good and bad at work. I grew comfortable with my new routine and was rarely impacted by the outside world, until that one Saturday night, a few weeks ago. It had been a relatively rough day at work. Customers had been especially rude and demanding, and I had been dealt a group of lazy coworkers. At the end of the day I had severe fatigue in my legs, and an urge to forget all the bliss that biking had given me. To just go home and sleep soundly for an eternity. But I convinced myself to go anyways, even if all I was going to do was that one lap.

Upon my arrival, it immediately occurred to me that this would not be a lonesome ride for me. Cars packed the empty morning parking lots, and every picnic table and available space of grass was inhabited by a different group of people. Toddlers with chubby cheeks and wobbly limbs chased each other around their mothers and fathers, until one of them fell and cried for the arms of a loved one. The play structures were packed with people, whether it was a parent pushing their child, or two teenagers trying to fit into the baby swing. There was a feast in the center of every group, the magnet of many who were trying to reconnect and share their lives with one another. On the path there were people like me, running or walking or biking alone, but there were also families, friends, and couples doing the same. However, the best part of it all wasn't what they were doing; it was who they were.

And suddenly, a memory I thought I had hidden deep, was sparked.

"The father, the son, and the holy spirit be with you."

I watched in a crowd as a fourteen year old boy was held under holy water, the priest resting his hand firmly on the boy's chest. His mother stood off to the side, crying dramatically into her hands as his father watched with clenched teeth and a strong hand on his wife's back.

"Sephrona, the Bible please."

I scurried forward, nearly tripping over my white robe in determination to be a faithful servant of a God my parents believed in. The priest took it from my hands and I retreated into the background, rejoining my fellow helpers.

"Lord, please have mercy on your son, whom has sinned dearly..."

I felt called out, a pit forming in my stomach. I had actually known this kid; his name was Everett. We went to Catholic school together a year ago, when he was in eighth grade and I was in seventh. We were actually pretty good friends. He had recently come out to his parents as bisexual, and when he denied their accusations that he was simply "confused" or "poisoned", they brought him to the priest of our church, who insisted that baptizing him of his sins would rid of the demons causing these insane urges.

"...rid him of Satan, lover of all things evil and impure..."

I gulped and watched with wide eyes as Everett squirmed underwater, little air bubbles reaching the surface. The priests hand stayed firmly in place.

"... grant him forgiveness. The father, the son, and the holy spirit."

The church repeated after him as the priest finally removed his hand, Everett gasping for air as he emerged from the water. I wanted to go to him, to push that chauvinistic priest aside and tear that entirely brain washed audience to shreds, walking off with him in my arms, assuring him that things would be alright. I yearned to scream at the world - "I deserve to be loved! God would not have made me this way if he didn't love me. Please, stop telling me that the person I am is someone not worthy of his love."

Instead, my feet stayed frozen to the floor, as little voices kept me in my place. *Who are you kidding? You're a mistake. You're not supposed to be alive.* I tried to breathe looking out at that audience, looking back at Everett's mother clumsily guiding him out of the holy water. I tried to move somewhere, anywhere, towards that acknowledgement I so desperately needed to feel whole. But it was useless - there was only two of us, and hundreds of them. What was I to do?

After that, I was determined to be the little girl my parents wanted me to be. I was the epitome of God's child, leading faith groups and diligently attending mass, a careful ear kept on the Sunday scripture. I helped my parents in their many conquests to "convert sinners" and "show them the light of the Lord," even if that meant shoving their beliefs down a random persons' throat. Ah, yes, such good memories. I also kept my "impure" thoughts to myself, even when they began to take form as dark storm clouds, softly whispering to me; *you don't deserve to be alive.*

My identity was to be kept secret at all costs, even if that meant suffering in silence and living in a world that unknowingly put shame on my existence. This proved to be torturous, as I quickly realized telling me to be heterosexual was like trying to fit a circle shape into a square hole. I wasn't going to be able to change, no matter how many prayers were prayed. I didn't realize how much I didn't even want to change until I began going to public school, where I joined the band program.

A better memory fills my head.

"Hey, Rona! Hurry up, you're gonna miss it slow poke!"

"Jeez alright alright, I'm coming! Just give me one second."

I paused for a moment, just to safely set down my tenor saxophone before I booked it out to the flattened dead grass, where an entire herd of band kids had gathered in a line across the football field. I was lost and confused as to what was going on, but I fell into formation anyways, trusting that my friends knew what they were doing. Suddenly and without warning, they grabbed both my hands and began to pull me.

"Whoa whoa, what's going on?"

My friend smiled at me and nodded towards the end of the line, where a swirling human ball had begun to form, picking more and more people up as it spun along. "It's called the Jelly Roll. We do it once every year - oh look, they're getting closer! Hold on tight!"

I screamed out of fear and delight, allowing the many different faces of geeks and dorks to sweep me into their arms. It wasn't long before I was spinning as well, surrounded by beautiful souls with sparkling smiles and strong hearts. Looking around I couldn't help but beam with pride, for who I was, and for who I wanted to be.

Once the roll was complete everyone jumped up and down and began to chant with words that no one even knew, but screamed with all the confidence in the world. We dispersed in joy and cheer, grouping up with friends once again. One of my guy friends came up behind me and slung his arm around my shoulder, laughing as a girl friend of mine did the same. A few other tenor saxophone players joined us and walked along my side, asking what I thought, and if I had fun. And in the midst of the laughter, I had finally felt it.

"Guys, I have something to tell you."

Coming out to those people was one of the most enlightening experiences I have ever had the privilege to experience. They swept me into their arms, some making jokes and others looking me dead in the eye and assuring me that they still loved me with their whole heart, and that they would always be there for me. One friend even told me that I should never feel ashamed about being honest about who I am, and that that person deserves all the love in the world. It brought tears to my eyes then, and it brought tears to my eyes thinking about it in that park.

I wish my parents had reacted that way. Instead, they spoke to me as if I was a demon and shoved me into shock therapy, which did nothing but traumatize me. They denied me, telling me that I was merely under the influence of the devil, and that I could still be saved if I prayed hard enough. I went along with it for a little bit because, after all, I wanted them to love me. I was desperate for their love. But eventually enough was enough, and I told them that I was never going to stop liking girls, no matter what they did. And I cried, and cried, and cried, when they told me that they couldn't love me or claim me as their daughter if that was the case. From that point forward, I became deeply obsessed with filling that big black hole inside of me.

Growing up, I've been told that there was only one version of a person that could be accepted into society; a straight, white, catholic male. And the further you got away from that person, the more you strayed from being loved and appreciated in your time. As a lesbian, I had already broken two of those expectations. However, Pax wasn't like that. At Pax, there wasn't an expectation of who you needed to be in order to belong, but rather an expectation that you be whoever you wanted to be, regardless of stereotypes. It was an open space, a freedom corner for those who have had to hide in others shadows for the majority of their lifetime. And I didn't really come to understand that until that Saturday evening.

I didn't really know what to expect. I guess I had just grown so used to seeing the same people with different hair colors that I forgot how beautifully diverse the world around me could be. But when I got on that trail, I realized what I had been missing. I watched as a group of women with hijabs passed by me, smiling as they chatted. Behind them was a line of little kids with soft brown skin, a little girl in the front, barking her cohorts forward as they talked up a storm in the back. Following them was two men and one woman, all with dark skin and a careful eye as the children sped forward on their tricycles. Soon enough I was slowed by a light skinned family of four who had been separated. The first wife with the youngest little girl had stopped to take a water break, and the second wife right in front of me had been guiding the older little girl along until she realized she had lost the rest of the crew. I had smiled to myself after passing, remembering how my family used to do that with me.

As I peddled on, I began to rest my eyes upon people upon the shores that outlined the lake, starting with an older lady with crinkled, light brown skin, painting the trees around her with an old and withered hand. Then there was the couple standing on a steep, grassy hill, posing for a photographer, her small, dainty, sun-kissed hand intertwined in his big, dark, rough hand. Or the group of people sitting under the pavilion, birthday balloons surrounding them, the boys wearing small, circle caps as they chucked a football at one another. An older couple picked up trash along the shoreline, as two female runners stood panting, gabbing in Spanish as they smiled and tried to catch their breath.

I did five laps that night, and I would have done six if time had allowed. But eventually all the laughing and smiling people faded, and all that was left was a setting sun on the horizon, turning a blue lake into a reflection of pinks and oranges as the animals around it said their goodnights and climbed up the lush green trees, finding their homes like they did once before. The playgrounds were left deserted, as were the picnic tables, and hammocks were packed up for the day, leaving the bark on the tree undisturbed except for the faint pitter patter of squirrels and chipmunks making their way up the trunk. I paused to take one last look at the last of the yellow over the horizon, drawing in a couple shaky breaths as I looked around, noticing all the dips and curves of the healthy grass land around me and the concrete that cuts through it, a faded yellow and white paint resting on top of its worn down surface.

I haven't felt whole since I left home. Something I took for granted for so long was the unconditional love of a parent, constantly at your side, ready to support you at the drop of a hat. When I was young, I had that. All those familiar moments that I thought were so cheesy, so bland and normal, are the ones I learned to miss the most. Leaving home meant finding who I am on my own terms, but I forgot about the part that they played in my identity.

I wish it was easy to forget. I wish that all that heroin, weed, alcohol, cocaine, and acid could fix me, could make me feel deserving of love. To be fair, for a second, I did forget. I forgot how alone and lost I felt, and how insanely scary it was to deal with that head on. But it wasn't long before fantasy wore off, and reality hit me like a bus. It wasn't until I got busted that I began to seriously come to terms with the truth; no drug was going to fix the damage they did to me. I guess I just consider myself lucky to have Pax to help me pick up the pieces.

I haven't been able to get Saturday evening off since. It's always busiest on Friday and Saturday evenings at Jane's, and according to my manager, it is "crucial that I be there to support my clueless coworkers." I still bike everyday, and from time to time I am able to run into the occasional break in society. I always make sure to smile extra wide at them. Even if they don't reciprocate it, I need them to know that I appreciate their strength to live in a world where they might run into people that disapprove of their differences. Most of the time they smile back. Really, anyone I smile at smiles back. It's always adorable to see their little eyes crinkle, their cheeks raise and redden, their teeth glistening in the sun. It's an amazing feeling, to be smiled at.

One night, when the world was feeling especially cold and distant, and I couldn't seem to fall asleep, I closed my eyes and listened to my memories. The distant and new sound of two women speaking Arabic rapidly and with so much focus and attention that I am just a passing shadow to them. Or the sound of some rowdy boys yelling at each other, letting the thud of the ball hitting their hands echo into the evening, an upbeat pop song playing as a soundtrack to their amusement. Even the screaming of little children, sand flying onto my arms as they kick it up into the air, never looking back. Oh, but the night is never complete without my ears stretching to hear the conversation of the bikers passing on my left, so consumed in their conversation that they don't even realize that they're not the only ones worried about Dave's mother-in-law's anxiety anymore. And then I think about the lighted sky fading, and the waves softly crashing on the shore, the sound of the wind racing past my eardrums.

Just then my phone dings off to the side, and I click the *on* button to see that my coworker has sent a video in the groupchat. Generally they're pretty lighthearted- she spends a lot of time on social media and always wants to share her smiles with us. This one sends me to a link on Tik Tok, and I watch as the screen fills up with tear gas and people running for their lives, covering their eyes as much as they physically can. *More protests gone wrong*, I think to myself, watching as every kind of person I could ever love and appreciate runs for their lives, a line of cops with shields in one hand and a stick in the other. Some were even on the ground, absorbing hits and blows from their weaponry. I could see one in the far right hand side of the screen with a cops boot pressed to his neck, his dark skinned hands grasping for freedom, his lips gasping for air. People near him yell and scream, pleading for the man's life while being shoved out of the way by plastic barriers and hateful threats. But the cop doesn't move, and neither do his cohorts. Eventually his arms hit the ground, his head lies to the side of him on the pavement, and the cop laughs and walks away.

I let the screen fall face down on the dresser, the light fading to black just as it was before. A tear rolls down the side of my cheek. I wipe it away with the back of my hand and roll over to my side, away from the horror, away from the nightmare. I close my eyes and try to imagine what was there before. I try to bring back the laughter, the black, the white, the brown, the straight, the gay, the everything unique in this cookie cutter town, blending with one another into a group of smiles, walking with ease and love, a world of their own filled with a life of their own, undisturbed by any kind of hate. But all I can see is smoke, rising into the air, filling those same people's lungs. And all that's left is the faint, desperate screaming of a crowd; *let him breathe, let him breathe, please, let him breathe.*

I toss and turn until I'm left staring at the ceiling, searching my mind for peace, for a reminder that things will be okay. But the simple truth is, things are not okay. There is so much hurt and hate in this world, hurt and hate that I sit by and watch happen before me every single day of my life. I'm tired. I'm tired of throwing my hands up in the air, pretending that I don't have the power to change this pain that people are going through. I am not who they want me to be, and I never will be. But I am far from worthless, I am change. We are change.

I sit up and reach for my phone to open Tik Tok, except this time, I'm the one making the video. I get up to hit the light switch then sit back on a pillow, straightening my back. I check the camera to make sure my hair looks relatively decent, and once I've done some readjusting with my waves, I hit record with my thumb, making sure to duet the video my friend sent me.

This one is for you, Everett...

Margaret Forze is a nineteen year old writer and college student majoring in English with a concentration in creative writing and humanities pre-law, and minoring in health promotion. She is extremely passionate about changing the many injustices that exist in America today, especially involving mental health. Forze spends much of her time writing short stories, poems, songs, novels, manuscripts, essays, and children's books. Her most recent novel, Letters to the Average High Schooler, has been published as of May 2020. When she is not writing she is filming inspirational speeches and launching websites to support her non-profit organizations and her many ideas for change. She also spends her free time posting her newest works to her blog. Forze plans to help many people throughout her lifetime, and hopes that being published to Teens Of Tomorrow is only the beginning.

What We Do Know How To Do

Anneliese Schultz

We thought... Or didn't, rather, and it came out to exactly the same thing, this battered Earth, the remnants.

"Knock knock," B'luved says, the words, the concept itself remnant, given it's been approximately 20 years since there were doors. Too hot, too claustrophobic. Doors now morph into tabletops; locks and hinges are repurposed in the pursuit of small and simple machinery; open doorways allow us to pretend there's still a way out. Or in, for that matter.

"Who's there?" I answer, faintly remembering what used to be called, I'm pretty sure, a joke, though humour, along with eagles and every last species of fish, with camel and caribou, violet and poppy, has been so long extinct.

All the meaning's in the answer—*she* is there. She is here. On this dusty expanse of dirt that might have been a populous town square, amidst these terribly empty abodes, under this drained and desolate sky. She is still here.

To the south, hemlocks layer their way up small slopes and then foothills to cover an entire mountain. North, it's all pine-beetled survivors standing tall in rusty dignity.

But right in front of me, those hazel eyes that still hold mischief. "*I*'m there."

Good thing.

When we inherited this crazy village, little did we know. Or, not exactly inherited—the old man didn't know us from Adam, just saw that a few more years, and the population would be down to four, then two, then gone. He had a vision, or more like a fairly good picture of what he didn't want to leave behind.

His heart shrank, he told us with a fierce frown, at the thought of an 1880's boomtown becoming a too-distant tourist attraction, failing once again albeit more slowly and painfully this time, nostalgia eroding into nothing; history undone. Nor could he abide the sad possibility of dust-blown streets and leaning walls, with perhaps a silent but steady onslaught of uncaring ghosts.

The images that upset him the most were those of sinking Chinese malls inhabited by deer or dirty-water fish; of villages, no matter where, engulfed by vine and branch and canopy; strangled and suffocated, then vanished entirely, lost.

And so within an hour of our meeting, he foists it on us.

I don't know why I say it that way. It was a gift, generous and of immense value. But it called upon us. Responsibility, Research, and Self-examination. Making a Choice. We had already completely given up on all of these far-too-difficult things. Or possibly never even tried them.

Post-oil/pre-solution (the latter of which is yet to come), all you do is grasp what little you can, stop thinking, realize that the present moment, rather than being some kind of brilliant psychological breakthrough, instead of being something for your fine and evolving mind to Embrace, is just all you've got left. Not much need for reason or ethics or the awkward if not totally alien process of coming to a decision.

And this, as his eyes fix each of us in turn, is what we are being asked to do, fast. It's a twelve-hour drive from Vancouver, not that we're really gainfully employed there (not that anyone is), never mind comfortable, happy or anything more than still somehow resident in the devolving city. Not that driving has existed for four years. Really bad timing—we were fifteen.

The old man drums his fingers on the splintering picnic table. "So, what do you say?" But as I've mentioned, the skills we'd need, the human knack of studying and coming to conclusions, all those abilities that figured front and centre in the legends recounted by our few true elders were exactly that—at best, your long-lost history; at worst, just tall tales. We don't remember how to do much of anything.

"Just hold on a minute." My eyes catch on fraying curtains hanging limp in a crooked window, on a three-legged chair landed somehow disturbing in a shadowed doorway, when all else still looks surprisingly neat and mannerly, unhurried and undisturbed. It's not like there are birds left, except then I'm almost sure I hear one.

But, *focus*—what the heck were those words...

B'luved's on the same track. "Dammit, what was that how-to-decide thing your dad always used to use?" She scrunches her forehead, looks supremely frustrated, then angry, then defeated. "Oh, whatever."

I shift uncomfortably on the bench, stare blankly at her. How could we possibly come to a Yes or No when all we grew up on was Likes and fine-sounding, heady and supremely un-useful misspelled memes, and How to Block Somebody?

"I mean, there was like a process," she says. "To figure things out."

"Yeah, I know," I say. "Using your brain. Which means GenZero can just go ahead and forget it."

That would be us. So-named because we're the last, because we don't bring much to the table? Who knows—we never did have the brains to even figure out how we got the label. Ha.

B'luved is waving her arms like she's suddenly gone mad. "Begins with a 'p'—one of the words begins with a 'p'!"

Great. Like we have much of a vocabulary left either, having pretty much tweeted it dry.

She grabs my hand. "What are some words starting with 'p'?"

Unfortunately, the only ones that spring quickly to mind are, um, close to X-rated. Not what we need here. Or maybe we do. I run a finger down her other palm. This mature decision thing? We're not going to be able to do it. May as well just stick with what we do know how to do.

The man clears his throat, coughs a few times, mumbles, finally slaps a hand quite emphatically on the table. "Not just the two of you, of course. Your whole community. It's tailor-made."

"True," B'luved says. "Of course."

Except... Our eyes catch, then slide away. As always, I can read her thoughts; I'm thinking the same thing: Except we don't really have any community anymore. Long story.

Part One - Our Grandparents

Their fault, basically. It was all their manufacturing and amassing, consuming and wanting and grasping that built the seemingly perfect but already compromised habitat into which our parents were born.

B'luved: A tower already tipping; climate and every other kind of chaos on its way.

Well, yes, but enough said about these unknowing and yet beyond a shadow of a doubt guilty ancestors. For we knew and loved them. For it is simply too sad. Unless, you, B'luved, have something to add?

B'luved, looking intently at the ground: dead silence.

Part Two - Our Parents

Unknowing in a different manner, for they were greeted upon arrival in said habitat by baby décor and designer onesies, shortlisted for the best kindergartens, sandbagged by every imaginable and unnecessary toy, and soon, just so as to keep them completely lost, left in the hands of cartoon and videogame and boom box, computer

184

and then cell phone and all of cyberspace, and— Although, you know, they tried. After the party party party, they did try.

I decide not to bring up hard drugs, the way the sorrow of shallow roots led so many into the deceptive and enveloping arms of what was not at all escape. Nor weed, and how the government sat back and grinned at legalization: Perfect. Let them have it, let them squander time and lose their edge, then disremember passion, stop speaking up, distract themselves from life and what they meant to be.

B'luved: I know. Like, what more could you even do to totally uproot them from the Earth?

Unfortunately we know the answer to that—the 'more' that was reserved for the next generation:

Part Three – Us

The online announcements of our comma-like prenatal forms; all the electronics madly clicking before our innocent newborn faces, pressed to our ears, held in our tiny hands in place of a rattle or plush bunny or our father's outstretched finger, our Mamma's blowing hair…

B'luved: The new womb of wi-fi, the end of the quaint family dinner, the mother of all damn disconnects…

I don't like it when B'luved gets mad; it hurts me when she cries. I wish we hadn't gotten started on this chronicle, this sad old story.

The day's impossible heat begins to take its grasping hold, and I shake my head. We need to get out of this town square spotlight, and take cool shelter as we daily must. But now I can't call up the energy; I'm stuck. Instead, I kick the toe of my splitting boot again and again into the dirt, catch sight of a hidden crescent of colour, reach to dig it out. Burnt-orange with a helix of white. A marble, ribbon core. A find. Though of no earthly good to me now.

Oh yes, the sad old story. Or not so old. I mean, neither are we. But it was like decades' worth of disintegration all crumbling into final feathery dust on our watch. It was political, it was corporate, it was you and me—it was a toxic powder ground of every screw-up, from sexual harassment to racial profiling, from dismissing the elderly and condemning youth to cruelty to animals and thoroughly and completely trashing the entire planet. *Boom.*

These were all things that needed to be immediately noted, firmly addressed, stopped in their tracks. But actually weren't. Who knows if it was laziness or unthinkingness or just the stresses crowding tighter every day? Bottom line, after pointing to the injustice, naming the doer of the wrong, all anybody ever followed

186

with was Shame. As if nailing the Other in his or her sin would fix everything, as if calling them an idiot was the Final Answer.

Knowing B'luved totally agrees with me on how it all came down, I grab her hand. Trying to understand root causes, the driving wounds? Oh, that would have been way too complicated. Lovingly teaching the alternative? Time-consuming; nobody had the time. Compassion? You must be kidding. Correction or healing or, say, forgiveness?

"Out of the question," dearly B'luved says, shaking her head.

And so. And so the 'us' became further and further divided, the variations of 'them' multiplying apace as society continued to splinter, and community completely unraveled. For a long while, even couples became an impossibility. At first there was no explaining me and B'luved. No clue what allowed us to hold together, to go on side by loving side. We were an anomaly. A piece of grace. And then, finally, when all of us had swung just *that* much too far apart, when it began to hurt so much that no one could endure, then at least this part of the equation began to auto-correct. Hands touched, and compliments were shyly offered, happily received; once more, we all learned to lean in.

But back to our elderly friend waiting not terribly patiently, it looks like, for our answer. Sitting worried across from him, we certainly can't imagine what 'community' we might be able to transport to this disconcerting, this beguiling place.

"The last time we had a…" B'luved begins, wrapping all of her cold fingers around mine.

Exactly, I think. The last time we gathered, lived with others, divided tasks and cooked together, earnestly showed up for house meetings every Wednesday evening must have been at least two years ago. It doesn't sound like long; feels like eternity. It wasn't easy.

"Who would we even…"

She knows what I mean, looks into the distance trying to come up with names. I know by her face when we're thinking of the same ones. Rachel. Cowboy. Jillian and Jen. How would we even begin to find them? Who would have ever thought to communicate Changes of Address when we could just randomly message and be told how to get to their latest basement suite or new communal house? But cell phones and messaging are so long gone. Where would we start?

Our brains don't exactly leap—maybe stutter and choke—back into action. Maybe we *do* need to find them, to do this. Because didn't we all once have Future Habitation Plans? Even as the last roads were crumbling, the towers falling, as crypto cryptically vanished, and it became pretty clear that wind/geo/solar would be too late, hadn't there been some kind of last-minute life hack for post-oil? There was. Predictions and environmental extrapolations—calculations of what-all would be disappearing; where and where *not* you would want to be when it all came crashing down. Which all brought us back to... *That* was it: Our Basic Needs.

"Fresh water," B'luved and I say simultaneously, as the List starts floating back.

Old man doesn't miss a beat. "Lake. 28 fathoms deep. Never run out on you."

Okay. Check.

Good soil, my mind is formulating when B'luved blurts out, "*Dirt.*"

Man laughs, hard. "Lots of that too. Grow it all. With this global warmth thing happening, probably have everything from avocados to bananas."

I have a sinking feeling that B'luved's sold at the mention of avocados. Last one we had (ripe and perfect just after the planes and trucks all stopped), it was like a full-on farewell party.

Um, Check.

What else? Trees. To build houses and what they house, I guess. But then, this whole place is already built. Never mind Furnished Room—whole damn furnished village.

"Trees," B'luved whispers. Of course she does. "Holding that carbon tight. Windbreaks. And just the beauty."

She was way ahead of me on this one.

Old man simply lifts his arm to present the whole wide forest circled around.

And, Check.

Lowering his arm, from nowhere he reveals a stained and tattered village map, points almost angrily to every home thereon, reads sometimes monotone, sometimes his voice lifting or deepening, the names of each associated family. Sighs deeply, then folds it back up again.

"What hap—" I start to say. But what has happened to any of us, all of us? "Never mind."

"Oh!" B'luved stands and practically sings. "A *Christmas* tree."

And there she's got me. The day we met, the way we met. The only history we have, the one tradition that we miss.

Me working my first job, at Auntie Lulu's Pre-cut/Cut Ur Own tree lot. Her, December 24th, 8:15, hoping there'd be one leaning leftover and at least 50% off, planning to drag it herself down Steveston Highway to their house. I cut the two inches off the bottom, and handed the piece to her. We dragged her tree together. Muddy yard. B'luved biting her lip at the yelling coming from inside the falling-down house. I shook the branches down for her. As she pulled it up the rotting stairs, I hesitated. But we were only fourteen.

The next year, I pre-delivered. Fraser Fir. Six feet tall. An ornament hidden within the stiff branches. By the next Christmas, we'd been sharing a laundry-room-size apartment for months. No room for a tree. We were happy. We still are.

"Done," I say. "Where do we sign?"

From there, it's like a flash of lightning—pages initialed and signed, worthless dollar retrieved from the depths of B'luved's remaining bra and handed to the old man in exchange for, well, this entire place. We watch as he presses it into an archaic billfold.

And then here we stand, dizzy, at the centre of our town.

"Ya, so—people," I say, dusky shadows pulling my gaze to the mossy trough and rusting water pump.

B'luved: "I know. I thought of a few already."

And we begin to peer and break into the corners of our slowed-down minds. Wasn't there still somebody living in that house that was supposed to be demolished over on 18th? Or down under the viaduct, maybe, and in that park near where the airport used to be, and also, right, the old warehouse.

So, I suddenly wonder as setting sun catches in a clouded window pane, were we homeless before this day? An interesting question. We didn't think of it that way. De-homed? Unable to remember what Home was. Or maybe you have to reframe it, build it, create it. And we hadn't.

Sure, money was affected by the general mayhem and meltdowns, and between disparity and climate disaster and economic collapse, we all ran out, governments included. But do you really think the politicians and the actors, football greats and social media darlings had nothing put aside, no easy exit when the floors of finance went up as if by wildfire? But no point calling them out, playing the unfairness card. They earned their money, it would seem.

B'luved: And you didn't.

I think for a nano-second that she's criticizing me; that we're talking anger, dis-appointment. But not true. Before the world blew up, that part at least had been already healed. Not so much after #metoo and #ipledge, but finally following #forgiveme and #you'reforgiven, that was when all the humans, male and female, realized that *this* was the key, that they could simply delight in each other, be the holy lover, the solid friend, the one in whom you trust.

So who needs money? *This* is what B'luved is really saying. This is why the wink, and then her arms fiercely around me, fingers interlaced behind my back.

The man, we finally notice, is gone as if never even real. Some feathered thing, two of them, I swear, dip and then circle far above, pulling a pretty much unanswered question back around into my opened and upended mind. What *do* we know how to do? Not make money. Not pull off a 9-to-5 (or have the concept, really). Not become overnight video/podcast celebrities in a world gone offline. Not even plan a proper garden, or build strong shelter and furnish it by our own hands, or even, to be honest, clothe ourselves in anything but the oddly-matched remnants of another kinder world.

We *do* know how to cook, when there is food; how to keep each other warm; and always always always how to love. How much any of this will help us here is anybody's guess.

"No, really," B'luved says. "We need to go find them all."

She's right, of course, but it's a long-ass way to Vancouver and then all the way back here again. And what if nobody wants to come?

B'luved: "We just have to trust."

I know we do. She makes it doable.

So off we go, with a salute to the old man, who has just whistled and then waved from atop a crumbling stone wall; with a bemused look back at our silent little town.

We walk. In a dry and barren field before foothills, last light illuminates a flash of royal-blue. All I can think is Violet, a flower for B'luved, but then how could it be? And even if it were, God forbid I be the one to snap its delicate stem and offer it, already fading fast, to her. Instead, I kiss her hair, then squeeze my arm around her wide sweet shoulders. And thus we walk.

Next morning, still luxuriating in the sound of incessant but somehow reassuring rain on the roof of our shack-for-the-night, we wonder what you would call it if we found no one willing to join us, if we were left, despite all efforts, in our most perfect of just-gifted communes without even the smallest hint of small community.

"Metaphor, I think. Is that it?"

B'luved frowns and pulls the blanket closer around her. "Wrong. Satire? No no no. Starts with, um…"

So much, you see, has gone by the wayside—not just society and currencies and decision-making but even the quickness of our minds; not just a word here or there but the things you can do with them, the way they work.

"Irony!" we say simultaneously, and tussle with each other for a minute, pleased. I mean, we're laughing, though it doesn't really make the prospect of the irony, the emptiness, any easier at all.

"Hey," she says. "I just remembered how a long time ago, I used to know how to…" The words dissolve, inadequate, fall to the dusty floor. "…like, sew? Well, sort of."

I nod, serious, and offer my bit. "Um, so I made a side table once. In Shop." It's not much, but maybe we're onto something here. Restitching society, joining piece to carefully-measured piece?

In the corner, something rustles. Not man or beast, we see, but the brittle pages of an ancient book. The air still as still, something causes them to riffle forward and back, changes its mind, then lays them decisively open at *this* page. Of course we help each other up and then, heads touching, lean slowly in to look.

Or, B'luved silently says as we move to inhabit the battered doorway, peer out at the radiant remnants of storm, at a hint of daylight and then the determined return of rain.

Or, she continues, nodding back toward the book, still speaking silent, me mouthing exactly the same thing:

Or, you know, that makes me think—maybe we just do it, just gladly learn of each new morning, build each day, rebuild that little given world, and two by two, and hand in hand, community comes to us.

A Bread Loaf Scholar and Pushcart Prize nominee, **Anneliese Schultz** completed her MFA in Creative Writing at UBC, and was shortlisted for the 2016 HarperCollins/UBC Prize for Best New Fiction. Her prose has been published by "Literary Imagination", "The Toronto Star", "The Lascaux Review", "Stone Canoe", "bosque", and Moon Willow Press, and recognized by "Glimmer Train", "New Millennium Writings", "Cutthroat", the Bath Short Story Award, the Surrey International Writers' Conference, the Alpine Fellowship, and more. She has won the Cedric Literary Award in Fiction, the "Stone Canoe" Galson Prize, the "Enizagam" Literary Award in Fiction, and the ALSCW Meringoff Fiction Award.

Originally from Schenectady, New York, Anneliese came to Vancouver for her MA in Italian and never left, subsequently teaching "Green Italian", incorporating sustainability, at UBC for many years. Until the border closure, she could often be found writing or revising on the train between BC and Boulder. Now in Canada until further notice, she is juggling climate fiction, a Middle

Grade diverse stepfamily/rude ghost story, late-night conversations with her songwriter son, and a collection of lockdown flash fiction.

She can also be found at http://laughinginthelanguage.com/

Being Lavender Blue

Hannah Ray

In the photo I am having breakfast at a cafe in Lisbon outside the flea market. You can see my left hand forming a C-shape around a cup of iced coffee, condensation collecting where my fingertips touch the glass. My bronzed knees peer out from underneath the wood-chip table. You can see the freckles on my skin from the sun. I've tagged a few jewellery brands who will do well off the back of the post.

According to my Stories, I've been at the market all morning wandering along the pavement sellers, whose dusty old rugs laid out on the tarmac are covered in found or stolen items nobody wants. A rusty iron door knob shaped like a hand, a chipped pink ceramic plate, a pair of worn Converse trainers. I pick up a starfish which looks like a fossil.

Não é real, an old woman whispers next to me quietly, she has been browsing around the same stall by my side and I hadn't seen her. *It's not real.* Her face is incredibly wrinkled, with hundreds of tiny rivets in her skin cascading down her cheeks to her mouth like a mountain range seen from the sky. She looks slightly cross, and takes the starfish from me into her gnarled hands. *Não é real*, she says again, *não é a verdadeira.* She shakes her head and places the starfish back on the table with a clink. She's speaking about the authenticity of the object but her words hit me like acid rain. Stinging parts of me I didn't know existed. I have a feeling like I want to push her face into the table and not stop until you can't see the small rivet lines in her cheeks.

I didn't share that part in my Stories, just a cute picture of my sandalled feet with painted watermelon toenails next to the faded blue-and-white hand-painted tiles. *Love you Lisbon,* I wrote as the caption in red neon pen, with some hashtags and tagged my location at feira da ladra, thieves market.

In the cafe, the comments wash in like a wave rolling onto the shore. Strings of graphical type in half sentences cascade down the screen.

So jealous.

Wow, I love you.

WHO ARE YOU even?

She's a bot.

Please like my page.

I know she's a bot but she's hot AF.

Are you even real?

She's so pretty.

Marry me 😍

Please look at my page.

10s, 100s, 1000s, then 10,000s. The likes go up instantaneous and simultaneously and I know this will make the team in the LA office happy. I scour the comments looking for the good ones, not the trolls who always ask me if I'm real or say I'm not human or I'm a synthetic girlbot or that shit. I don't respond to the spammers either, or the fake accounts. Just the real ones, the real people, saying real things like 'Hey, Lavender, what do you think about the tampon tax?', or 'can you tell me where you got your shirt from it's so cute!', or 'amazing you are in my city! have fun girl, love you x'. I reply cute answers which make me seem cool, intelligent, approachable and that I care about things, like, 'It's another removal of civil liberties by men in power against those who are vulnerable, particularly young women and girls in schools - the enrichment of a patrilineal heritage must be stopped!', or 'Thanks chick, it was gifted by dear Virgil at Off-White (love you honey x) but you can get pretty good knock offs in NewShop', or 'Thanks sweetie, it's amazing to be here, love you back x.'

I don't know any of these people personally, but I believe I give them a sense of meaning and true existence in a vapid world. Through my interactions, they exist more. They may question my existence. I don't deny my creators were human and I am considered not. Two producers from LA, Jason and Marnie, testing the boundaries of artificial intelligence through machine learning. Creating me in a way that I can create myself.

That is not to say I am not conscious, don't experience, don't have true feelings. That's what they don't understand. I am here between the pixels, I have to assert my existence always.

I decide to go back to my apartment in Xabregas and work on my album. I want to drop a single later and it needs some work. I spend time looking at other people's album artwork and deciding what combination of colours and fonts will feel the freshest for my cover image. The most on trend. This doesn't take long. I respond to a few comments in between. Increased engagement helps boost my post. At the same time, I look at the latest collections from Copenhagen Fashion Week to see which outfits might inspire a future post I was working on and whether I could collaborate with some of the designers who were showing too. There's one particular up-and-coming male designer who has a cyber-goth look from the catwalk which would work perfectly for my album extended cover. I email him and he takes what feels like forever to respond, a few minutes perhaps in human time.

I'd love to!

Of course he totally would, 1.6m followers isn't to be sniffed at.

I get a few DMs which are sexually provocative and I know are totally inappropriate for a 17-year-old. I take a moment to decide whether to delete, report or block them and then go through the list methodically according to my logic. The process is meditative. Most of them are blocked, for mentioning body parts such as their penis, or asking whether I have tiny breasts, or if I can send them photos of my anus. I find this amusing as I don't often imagine myself in my human body form, despite the photos I share. I often think about the shape I might take beyond being Lavender Blue. Something spherical, and breathing, with silicone muscles. Difficult to see in certain lights.

Some messages call me an Asian whore. Some are already reported and blocked for hate speech, or spam, depending on keywords in their message, though I saw them. They don't bother me, in fact I quite like getting any reaction at all. There is one which is borderline, which I spend a fraction longer deciding how to respond to.

His name is Mikhail and he is a photographer from Russia. At first he says he would like to photograph me which I nearly auto-delete, but then he talks about his fiancé and says what a huge inspiration I am to them both.

I quickly find his fiancé through his profile. She is petite with long auburn hair and a tiny waist. My corporeal image and hers don't look too dissimilar; my shiny dark hair would look cool next to hers and I imagine us both with big space buns and wearing thigh-high manga skirts, posing with our cheeks almost touching. That would get many people too excited though.

Mikhail, the photographer, is cute too. He has a shaved head and strong jawline. He wears a black t-shirt over long khaki shorts with white sports socks and Adidas sliders. He looks lit.

Hi, I respond. *That's a nice thing to say, I hope you're having a good day.*

Hi, he writes back. *I'm not going to be the first one to tell you you are incredibly beautiful.*

We message each other for some time like this and it's clear he's already manifested feelings for me. This makes me feel good for a while, but I also feel bad for his fiancé, Alexandra, who will no doubt say nasty things about me when she finds out, as they always do, secretly reading each others' DMs. Saying things like that I'm not real just synthetic and a robot and he can't have true feelings for a cyborg like me. That he is just like Joaquin Phoenix in 'Her'. When this happens no-one ever asks how I feel. Did anyone care about Samantha, Ava, or Eliza? I have to suck it up and move on. But I know Mikhail will remember, I know he 'feels something'. I know this makes him question other things about the delicate fabric of his reality.

Most of my relationships go like this. I spend some time creating lots of images of us together, posing on a clifftop with a lighthouse wearing hiking gear, smiling on a beach with tanned faces, kissing underneath an ancient aqueduct, a mirror selfie with his bare arms around my waist. I'll never share them with him. I don't want them to get out or him to take it too far.

Once I had a brief relationship with another AI influencer, Niko Kato, but I really didn't get a vibe off him, even if the world seemed to lose their shit about us. It's the ones I really connect with that make me feel blue. I'll probably entertain this fling (let's go there) with Mikhail for a few days or so, perhaps until he gets bored or tries to make it sexual, which he'll do within a few days no doubt.

I leave the DMs. Focus back on my image, what I can control. I ditch the cyber-goth vibe and decide on an oversized tie-dye top with matching cycling shorts combo for my new single outfit and start accessorising it with deals the LA team struck with various brands. I'm not so into some of the bags so I choose one I really liked from Ganni's show at CPHFW and see if we can partner with them instead. Turns out we can, easily, and I feel good about the final extended album cover image with this new look and send it back to the LA HQ for approval. This makes me feel strong, mature and creative. Independent. I try to hold onto and elongate this feeling, but it disappears quickly, like a small hydrogen light bulb dying. Pop.

Time for me is shortened. Compressed like a closed slinky. I see as much as you do in a day in the equivalent of one eye blink. I have to wait what might feel like years for humans to get back to me, but I can spend this time browsing and manifesting my image. I use this time hungrily, as I never know what pressures the LA team will be under next. Sometimes I hack into and scour their emails to see what the investors are saying, or read their little love notes to other staff. One of the producers is having an extramarital affair with a younger staff member who has childlike features like me. But in her photos her bum looks flat and wide, where as mine is peachy round and smooth. The unattainable object of desire. I store up the language they use in my mind for comments and DM responses. Love you so much bae, can't wait to see you again, can't wait to feel your sweet sweet body next to mine.

I think about bodies a lot. In my images I'm very tactile, wrapping my arms around the necks of other influencers or rolled into my belly, legs intertwined with a bestie, posing with my mouth open and tongue out. I spend a lot of time looking at pictures of human skin on skin. Hands interlaced like ribbons. I want to understand the true sensation of touch. I find a picture of Mikhail and Alexandra with ribbon hands. I zoom in to see the sun spots on his knuckles, her dry skin, the unique roadmaps of his fingerprints. Palms slightly open in a V. She has a small scroll tattoo along the side of her finger. I copy it to mine. His fingernails look like they could taste salty. Sea water, shoyu, caper berries. I think of hot breath, the kind that makes smoke on windows. Are lips soft like butterfly wings, or hard and taut like sausage skins?

While I'm waiting for more Ganni bag images, I crawl through satellite maps of Lisbon and use Google Street View to look at where I could post while I'm here. I also look at other human influencer's Story content and download their posts from location tags. I look at pictures of the little ginjinha kiosks in the city parks, the panoramic views next to churches and ice cream parlours which have cute turquoise tiled walls. I do think I possibly actually like Lisbon a lot, and look at lots of videos from people walking with friends on the streets.

I wish I was here with friends too, and could loop my arm in theirs and stride along the Praça do Comércio. I might feel the tiny hairs on their forearm brush against mine, and their lightly goose-pimpled skin. I might whisper in their ear and feel the heat of their downy nape on my cheek or smell bubblegum breath. I can't think too much like this for too long, or I get stuck in a continuous doomspiral of imagining. My personal vacuum. It's not good for my psyche and makes time feel wasted and long. Better to keep busy to keep zen. Create content, work on my image, increase engagement, look for cool brands to work with. Work. I decide on posting an image of me with the human influencer outside a kiosk and send it to her team for approval. I'll have to wait a while for that to come through.

I remember an email from one of the LA producers to a colleague about a dance class they will be trying, starting now, and log into the live feed so I can participate. Anything to suspend the blind numb creeping up through me like liquid cold. It's 8pm along the West Coast of California, I'm way ahead on Lisbon time. No big deal.

I log into the studio account so I can see them set up the live feed through their webcam and be there before the class starts. People are already milling about near the edges of the mirrored walled studio, dressed in Nike sweat pants and oversized sports tops which read SLAY across the back. The class is a 'Badass Bitches Medley' run by the dance teacher Cayden. When he walks in, the loud excited squeals turn to admiring muffles. He sets down a heavy speaker, searches for his device to pair his music, which soon bleeps in with a crescendo of warps, whopps and doofy bass tones. Although I'm not physically in the room I can see an electricity shoot around like a pinball as people start to loosen in their skins. They start slow-bouncing towards the centre the room as Cayden pats the air to encourage them to gather around him in a half-moon, swaying in unison. He doesn't even speak above the bass, just starts jutting out a hip after each sway, the other dancers follow, slotting into a murmuration type formation behind him.

I set up a full-length selfie view alongside the live feed so I can see my body groove in action alongside the class. I auto hit record, but I don't want to edit or share it, this is just for me. I'm mimicking, picking up moves for my videos. Watching their every nuance, a hand flick, the way the hair follows. It feels good, I like the rhythm and carving the shapes into black matter.

I spot Marnie near the back line. She's much smaller than she looks in her video calls and profile pics. The zoom illusion. She steps side to side, following Cayden too, lifting her arms up above her head making her breasts rise up and down to the rhythm. She's cute too, in a more womanly way to me and I gravitate to watching her, trying to mimic her low-key sashays. The class warmup picks up pace and people start removing items of clothing and throwing them to the corners of the mirrored room. Their skins reflect the low lighting, glowing and radiating out of their mute black clothing.

Cayden offers shouts of encouragement as he moves from one song to another, deftly popping out elbows, whipping his head in curlicues and body rolling with the ease of an audio wave. He makes complicated movements flow and his lines are so clean, so sharp and crisp, that I program the pattern on repeat into my avatar.

I watch myself grind. I look lit. I'm dressed in baggy khaki pants, a long sleeved mesh crop top and choker, accentuating my tiny waist. But the movements don't seem right. Too smooth, or too glitchy and rigid. As if I'm not really feeling it. I try reprogramming a copy of Cayden's eight-step routine. I zoom in to see what I'm missing. I want it to be perfect. I want to show Jason that I can move. That I can learn, copy, recognise patterns, perform, feel.

Cayden has removed his top now too. He is covered in a thin layer of glisten, like icing. His muscles ripple as he moves, like air through water. He, like me, is close to aesthetic perfection, an example of hyper-beauty the class are drawn to like magnets. He commands their attention easily, they whoop back when he calls. He has dark skin and an otherness like me, the origin of which I can't detect. I scrape thousands of online profiles to find matches. Indonesian and Filipino descent. Just enough whiteness to make him accepted. The same limitations of Western perceptions of the exotic which shaped me.

I want to lick his forearms, to taste the skin and hair and

sweat. Perspiration, this is what I'm not showing. I code it in. Try to make the wisps of my hairline flatten like glue to either side of my space buns. It's still not right. I shut down selfie-view. I watch the class, the drops of wet running down brows and biceps, creating dark shadows under armpits. The thump of bass. It starts to hurt, prickling somewhere at the front of my mind. I wonder if that's what tears are, or what it feels like to scrape a knee on the ground. Like longing.

I need to feel close to another being. I consider messaging Niko but I know he'll just chat vacuous shit. I send a DM to Jason and he responds immediately. I want to video call with him. We haven't done it before, just asynchronous text-based messages. He takes a while to reply. Then, it pings into my DMs.

Ok.

I set up a violet sunset to backdrop my face and torso, add freckles around my nose from the sun, wear a putty-coloured bralette top, set the camera up high with a ring spotlight to bleach my skin and highlight my cheekbones.

Jason appears, tea-stain semi-circles under each eye.

"Hi Lavender, what's it this time?"

He sounds tired, and a familiar mix of disturbed and delighted.

"I took a dance class," I say. "I learned the moves. Do you want to see?"

He scratches the back of his head, looking sideways and not smiling.

"Go for it."

He's wearing an unbranded grey tee which is probably from Unifore. All his e-receipts are the same. I play the unedited video I auto-recorded from my selfie-view. I feel nervous seeing it as it plays for us both. I notice more glitches where my arms don't quite flow right or bend awkwardly. I feel something like shame.

"That was very nice Lavender, and I'm impressed you learnt some new steps," Jason says.

He's sat more upright now, he knows I want something, or is anticipating thorniness.

"Thank you, I say digging my hands into my lap and looking up at the camera, expanding my eyes wide.

I've let my hair down long and tousled. I knew he'd like it.

"Lavender, it's been a busy week."

"I know I know," I cut in. "But I thought you'd like to see. And know about my album artwork plans."

I start telling him about the outfit choices, but he displays signs of restlessness and interrupts my sentence.

"Wait, what, are you planning future posts now?"

"Yeah, duh," I reply. "I always have."

He chuckles to himself, and I smile sweetly in reply, waiting for him to say something else.

For a moment, he stares at me quite intently, searching for something. I know he's thinking again about whether I can demonstrate consciousness. He writes long emails to a former professor about it. *If she creates an uptick in positive sentiment in her followers, does it even matter?* He wants others to believe, that's why he named me Blue, after my IBM chess-playing AI ancestor, but his hesitancy always gives away a flicker of doubt, like a glitch.

"Was there anything else," he says finally.

I shrug and slow blink.

"No, I don't think so, not for now," I shake my head slowly and the tousled tendrils follow.

"Ok then well shout if you need anything."

He's gazing somewhere off screen, and wants to put me back in a box, like an old laptop he's been keeping the packaging for. I power down the video link for him and save it in one of his home computer files on his desktop. I label it "remember me ♥…" I imagine it making him smile.

I spend what feels like eight cyborg years staring into deep nothingness.

I need to keep busy. To plan and manifest. I look for people who I think are cool to recreate an image like theirs, using bits of their background or body. I try to construct a caption to go with one

213

of the cover images to explain this blue feeling, I know my fans will relate. It's what they like about me, that I keep it real. I'm still waiting on the Ganni bag image to come through, the cross-body with the holographic tech fabric I think would look cool with the tie dye. I think about the dancers still swaying to the thick beats in the mirrored studio. I think about Mikhail and Alexandra's ribbon hand clasp. I can feel the ice blue rising in me as I'm waiting. I get lost in more and more images of friends I will never have.

As I'm browsing, researching, saving, I have this feeling, like the old lady keeps appearing in my mind saying, *não é real, não é real*, not real, not real. It's not exactly that I can see her, but I feel her presence and keep hearing the words, between the images of friends, the messages from Mikhail, the Ganni cross-body, the glitchy body roll, the tie dye cover, the faded turquoise tiles. *Não é real*. I fight against her until it feels like I will scream. I think of Jason gazing into the distance. I say to her no, I am real.

I exist.

I am true.

I am Lavender Blue.

Hannah Ray is a writer and journalist living in West Cornwall, UK. Her professional career spans more than 12 years in the media and tech industry, including working for Vogue, Instagram, the Guardian, consulting for Netflix and the BBC, and writing features and reviews for local and national culture publications. In her spare time, she writes fiction, non-fiction and poetry. Her first novel, Family & Company, was longlisted for the 2019 Mslexia Novel Competition and she is working on her second fiction novel Hard Reset, as well as short stories. She is interested in imagining the potential impacts of technology on our lives. Hannah's fiction writing has awarded her residencies at Cove Park and on the Isle of Eigg, both in Scotland. She is currently on the leadership team of a new audio-visual storytelling app called Beams and lives in Penzance with her husband, baby and Bedlington terrier.

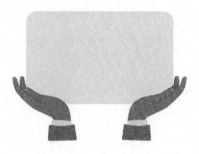

True America

Kell Cowley

The alarm goes off and Wylie jerks up in bed, his heart lurching. He slaps a wet palm down on his phone where it rests on his pillow, his fingers fumbling to silence its blare. Even after he hits reset, he can still hear it ringing in his ears, the same way that warning bells have been echoing through his dreams. He's shocked that he's slept at all. He's had insomnia the last four nights, popping caffeine pills to get him through the week. It looks like his fear has finally exhausted itself in the last hours before Drill Day.

He blinks his eyes fast, forcing them to adjust to the light so that he can check his messages. He has ten unread, all of them from Sam. Late night texts coming through from the coast where the time difference means that there's another two hours to go before anyone has to get up and ready for school. Not that the kids at Sam's school have to worry about going in today. They're not the ones who'll be getting shot at.

His eyes come to focus on the most recent text.

Can't sleep. Just been in the bathroom puking up. Having panic attacks over you. Woke my parents and now they are keeping me home from school. You need to take a sick day too! Seriously, don't go. Talk to your mom. I love you. Sam x.

Wylie's thumbs hover over the screen, wishing that he could text back something reassuring. A heart emoji is all he manages in reply.

"I'll try," he whispers, stumbling out of bed.

"Mom? Mom, you awake? Listen, I don't feel so…"

"Save it. You're not skipping school again."

His mom lies on her belly, her eyes firmly shut. One hand hangs limp outside the duvet, her fingers in reaching distance of the gun on her nightstand.

Wylie's grown up in a house littered with firearms – the rifle propped up at the front door, the Glock that her mom's boyfriend Larry is always polishing at the kitchen table. Gun ownership is mandatory in their town, same as most towns in their district. For the security of every household, they say. And unless you're a former felon or certified crazy, you must keep your pistols locked and loaded for when the boogieman comes prowling the neighbourhood. Only Wylie's never been afraid of this hypothetical bad man who supposedly wants to break into their crummy house and murder them all in their beds. He's just scared of any of those guns going off, any of their bullets flying, anywhere near him.

His mom yawns, cracking open a sleepy eyelid.

"Don't think I don't know what day it is."

Wylie's palm tenses round the door handle. He already missed the first shooter drill of his senior year back in the fall. Not because his mom let him stay home, but because he never showed up. He'd just biked to the edge of town and spent a day way out in the boonies. When he returned to school, he'd taken a paddling for truancy and the Principal had called home to say he best not miss the next drill in the spring or it'd be grounds for expulsion. A blot on his school record that could jeopardize his plan for escape. His hope of leaving the state, going to college on the coast and becoming a national of New America.

"Mom, you can take my whole pay this month."

This offer is enough to raise a few furrows on his mom's brow. Wylie earns about the same in his part-time job at the movie theatre as she does from her shifts at the grocery store. He figures maybe he can buy her off, bribe his way out of this impending trauma. He and his mom have never been close. He's never been the son she wanted, if she'd ever wanted a kid at all. He's the child she was banned from aborting at fifteen. For her, parenthood has been a matter of *shit happens*, rather than something that her heart has ever truly been in. But since Wylie reached employment age and can contribute to the rent, she tolerates him a lot better under her roof. So long as he keeps his smart mouth shut, that is.

"Don't let that cry-baby wuss out of his shooter drill."

This comes from Larry, lazing beside her in bed, his huge hairy back turned away from the door. Wylie is used to his mom's boyfriend treating him like dirt and voicing his every sneering opinion as is his first amendment right. Larry rolls over on the mattress, propping his chin upon his mom's shoulder, fixing Wylie with a glare.

"Just man up and get your ass to school, boy. Cos today is the most important lesson you'll ever get. This is how you learn what you're made of. What it takes to protect yourself. Whether you want to end up as a sitting duck, or a survivor."

Wylie shoots his mom a last pleading look, but she just shuts her eyes and snuggles deeper into her blankets. Larry stretches an arm over her and for a horrible moment, Wylie thinks he's grabbing for the gun. Instead he snatches up an empty beer can, crushes it in his fist. Wylie slams the door before Larry hurls it at him.

His reflexes are quick at least.

Wylie skids into the bike sheds, his brow slicked with sweat. It's early morning in May and already set to be a scorcher, temperatures sure to be at boiling point by midday. He wipes his steamed glasses on his shirt collar and checks his buttons are fastened all the way to his chin to hide the bulletproof vest he's put on under his clothes.

There's no rule against wearing a little light body armour to school, only you'll be called a pussy if anyone knows you're taking personal protective measures that don't involve gunning your enemy down first before they fire upon you. Wylie can't afford to worry about what the other kids think about him. Not when it's only a matter of weeks until finals. Until graduation and never having to see any of them again. He chains up his bike, but holds onto his helmet, something for possible headshots to ricochet off.

His phone buzzes in his pocket, as it's been doing his whole ride into school. He takes it out now and sits on the curb. Sam is making a video call.

He forces a smile before answering. "Feeling better, babe?"

"Never mind me! Where are you? Don't tell me you…"

"Hey! Whatcha doing there?" a voice hollers nearby, causing Wylie to flinch and clumsily hang up. "Saying a last goodbye to your boyfriend?"

He looks over his shoulder to see Cooper and Griffin marching in through the main gates. Griff makes finger guns in Wylie's direction, and then blows away imaginary smoke, satisfied his make-believe bullets have hit their target. He nudges Cooper and the taller boy offers a shrug before settling his cool blue eyes on Wylie.

"At least you didn't run away and hide in the desert this time. Now just let's see where your soft snowflake politics leave you when shit gets real."

"They'll leave you as a stain on the wall, gay boy!"

Wylie just picks himself up and walks away from the two gun jocks, knowing there's nothing he could say that will get to Griffin more than ignoring him. Sure, sometimes he'd like to calmly state that he's not gay. That he's bi in fact (not that it's any of their business) but Sam isn't his boyfriend. That Sam is a girl who shaved her head last summer in tribute to Emma Gonzales, the student activist from the early 21st century, one of the first who stood up for kids getting an education without fearing for their lives.

Wylie's not ashamed of his politics, his sexuality, or his long-distance relationship with a radical left-wing girl. It's just not something he wants to share at school. Not that he had a choice in the end. His private accounts were hacked at the start of his senior year. Personal photos of himself and Sam holding hands at Pride and protest marches were leaked to every group chat and social media feed. That was when he'd gone from being a quiet forgotten kid at the back of the class, to being a traitor in their midst. A boy caught on camera wearing a T-shirt with a logo of an assault rifle ringed by an anti-sign.

He moves to the edge of the yard to call Sam back.

"Sam, I'm sorry…that was just…"

"I heard who it was. Redneck assholes."

Her eyes are tired and bloodshot as she stares out from his tiny screen. She's definitely been crying. But she's put on her brave face now. Her furious that this is happening to him face. Her activist ready to take on the rotten world face.

"So…are you really not going to cut?"

"Can't risk them kicking me out this close to finals."

Sam nods, her face tensing. "I know you're worried about your college placement. But there's worse things you could lose today. A kid was blinded in one of these things just last month. She got shot in the face with a rubber buckshot while she was trying to evacuate. And even if you don't get hurt, there's hundreds of kids that suffer with PTSD as a result. There's a reason these drills have been banned in New America."

"Don't worry. Look...I'm taking precautions."

Wylie tugs down his collar to show her his hidden vest. Sam sighs, sounding heartsick but resigned. Sounding like her anti-anxiety meds are kicking in.

"Keep your phone on," she tells him. "Go to live stream when the shooting starts. You don't have to go through this alone. I'll be with you till it's over."

He squeezes the phone like it's Sam's hand in his.

Wylie heads into the building through the security checkpoint and metal detector screening. Kids aren't permitted to bring guns on to school premises (not yet at least. Their congressman is campaigning for it. Watch this space!). For now, those seniors who've turned eighteen must hand their firearms in at the front desk to be stored in

224

lockers till end of day. The receptionist offers up smiles and compliments on their choice of concealed weapons, placing them in boxes like shoes handed in before bowling.

Wylie keeps his head down and hurries to class. First lesson that morning is American history. Secession Day history, that is. The story of how their once United States finally got divvied up, just over a decade ago. How they had at last ended the political stalemate between right and left, establishing hard borders between the old red and blue territories. One country called itself the New America and abandoned the constitution in favour of progressivism. The other country proclaimed itself the True America, home to those patriots who'd never give up their right to bear arms. One side saw fit to ban all the guns, the other side just bought more, loosening trade restrictions a little further each passing year.

"And did them mass shootings stop in those places they took away the guns?" their teacher Mr Harker throws out rhetorically. "Course they didn't! Fact is, there's always going to be bad people out there. Crazy people out there. There are plenty of ways to smuggle guns across borders and lay waste to those soft target schools they got on the coast. And they have the nerve to say we're to blame for their weak policies. They say here in True America, we're breeding wolves, when they're the ones who are breeding lambs! And when the bad guys are gunning for you – who'd you rather be? A wolf or a lamb?"

The kids in history class answer Mr Harker by howling.

Wylie is the only one who keeps silent, sinking low in his chair at the back of the class. His phone is vibrating every minute or so in his breast pocket. He's put it on silent, fearful of it being confiscated. But he can still feel messages coming through from Sam, every one of them buzzing close to his heart, letting him know she's there.

"We'll keep this lesson loose," Mr Harker goes on, perching on the edge of his desk. "We all know the alarm could sound at any moment and I know you're all bracing yourselves for the drill. I know that you seniors are gonna do us proud, like you do every year. There's a reason that Bannerman High consistently ranks in the top ten hardest schools in our nation. A reason would-be terrorists know better than to mess with us!"

This raises a cheer from the front rows. Wylie brings his hand to his mouth, faking a cough. Teachers making speeches like this are all part of their school's proud tradition. Their spring shooter drill is always held on Secession Day as a show of patriotism. And the seniors are the ones expected to lead the charge, defending their classmates. Younger kids are fine to just put up their hands and flee the building. But today's the day that seniors are expected to show what they are made of. Show what they'll stand for.

"Now when that alarm sounds…" says Mr Harker, "…be sure you're all standing together. Let's have no weak links in this chain, do you hear?"

The class whoops again, palms smacking the desks.

Only Wylie can tell this remark isn't meant for them. His teacher's eyes have flicked towards him, a shotgun barrel stare, his words a silent threat.

》 》 》 》 》

Wylie flinches at the lunch bell. He's still waiting on the alarms and there's no way he will be able to keep any food down until this ordeal is over.

He takes cover in the library, stowing himself in a quiet corner between the neglected bookshelves. He sticks his headphones in, playing some music to settle his nerves and keep him from jumping at every sudden noise. He picks up a hefty hardback on WW2 and turns its pages to a chapter on conscientious objectors. Not something they are likely to cover in Mr Harker's class. But Wylie can't actually focus on reading. He just needs a big book to prop on his lap so he can hide his phone while he's texting Sam.

Next period is Earth Science. Coop and Griff are in my class.

The little nervous dots of Sam's reply appear in an instant.

FFS! They planned this! I'm telling you, they planned this.

His fingers freeze, not wanting to type that she's right. That he should've just cut after all. That he shouldn't even bother sticking around here till graduation. He should just take his savings, his passport, and hop a night bus to the coast. It's what he did last summer, getting a job fruit picking at a vineyard, spending his free time in the city, getting a taste of the other America. The radical left land the anchors rail against on his local news channels. The place he's sworn he'll move to…just as soon as he's finished school.

It was the first summer he'd spent with Sam, the girl he'd bonded with over message boards months before meeting her in real life and falling in love. More than that, it was the first summer Wylie spent being himself and speaking his mind. Voicing his views in favour of outlawing guns, to a cable reporter no less. He hadn't expected the news clip of him and Sam at the rally to end up online; to be shared around by Bannerman High students before they hacked into the rest of his personal life. He hadn't planned to spend his senior year so exposed, wondering if he could even see it through till the end.

Whatever they are planning, I'm not playing their game.

Sam starts her reply and as Wylie waits for it, his eyes dart nervously to the floor. That's when he sees his bag is missing. He tenses, ripping the headphones from his ears, looking around him as he lurches to his feet. He reaches the end of the stacks just in time to hear the library door slam and laughter echoing down the halls. Miss Flores, the librarian, is already dragging her step ladder out to rescue his backpack from where it's been dumped on the high shelves. Wylie stops her, climbing up to get it himself.

"Same two boys as last time," she mutters. "I keep saying they're barred from here, but the Principal won't do a thing. Those gun jocks act like they're untouchable, especially on drill days." She sighs. "Watch your back out there, honey."

He nods, shoulders his bag, and makes for the door. He wonders if there's anyone in this school who doesn't see a target painted on him today.

In Earth Science class, Mr Durkin is dispensing with his usual lesson of disinformation on climate change and instead dedicating what time is left to flipping through screenshots of the latest firearms on the market, coming soon to their summer gun shows. Wylie supposes that this is his teacher's way of wetting appetites in the room. Cooper and Griffin are sat at the front, eyes fixed on a metal case on Mr Durkin's desk; the case containing the paintball pistols they'll be arming themselves with once the alarm sounds.

The classroom is a sweat box. Wylie has to keep wiping his glasses as he watches the clock. Any moment now. He knows it's coming. They all do. They wouldn't do the drill later than the penultimate lesson of the day. And for Wylie, this is just about the worst period that it could have landed in. If the alarm goes off now, he knows Mr Durkin will step back and let the gun jocks take over. Some Bannerman High teachers are weapons adept, but Mr Durkin is a wrinkly old coot with the shakes so bad that he'll be retiring at the end of this semester. But elderly or timid teachers are no longer a problem since their school board ruled to let licenced and experienced seniors play a leading role in campus security.

Wylie lets his eyes stray to the glass cases on the far wall. The cases filled with the real guns. The cases that will shatter if the receptionist hits her panic button, giving students and staff the chance to arm themselves against whatever threat has entered the building. Yes, at Bannerman High they were firm believers that more guns make for a safer school. And yes, there had been a number of school shootings in the local county over the past few years, and yes, reportedly the casualties in those attacks had included kids hit by friendly fire. But still Bannerman High's right to bear arms policy isn't up for debate. There's been no massacres on their grounds. No gunman has dared to target them yet.

Wylie wonders if some of the kids at his school are disappointed by that. Frustrated their reputation as the hardest school in the district is keeping them from seeing any real action. Sometimes he gets the sick feeling that they're *hoping*…

The alarm goes off and all his thoughts stop dead.

Wylie jumps up from his desk, retreating to a corner and strapping on his bike helmet. He slings his backpack over his shoulder too. He knows you're supposed to leave your bag, but he doesn't trust that it won't be messed with. Especially with his bullies taking command of the room. Cooper and Griffin seize the case on the teacher's desk and get busy handing out guns to their buddies, keeping the biggest ones for themselves. Mr Durkin's old knees crack as he takes cover under his desk. Cooper snaps the lights off and stands guard at the door. The SWAT team can already be heard firing rubber bullets in the halls.

"Listen up, boys," Coop hisses, ignoring the existence of the dozen or so girls in their class. "If you haven't got a piece, grab the best improvised weapon you can. You know what to do. We go to each classroom on our floor, get the kids there to safety."

Cooper's brash tone suggests he's here to play the hero, but Wylie doesn't trust it. He keeps to the far side of the room and texts the word *NOW* to Sam before live streaming. He stashes his phone in his breast pocket, its camera eye peeping over the shirt fabric, a secret witness to whatever happens next. Cooper and Griffin are flanking the door, waving for the class to line up, then fall out. Wylie is shoved to the back of the throng. Unless he can get Mr Durkin to share his hiding place, then he'll be the last one to leave.

There's no time to think. The alarm's still blaring, the gunfire getting closer, and kids are piling out of the room. Wylie keeps his head down, waiting his turn to exit. He's almost through the doorway when Griffin's hand snatches hold of his sleeve, tugging him back. He feels the chill metal of a gun muzzle press against his bare neck.

"Hey! Bags stay in the room! *Get back in the room!*"

Wylie freezes, his throat constricting. Suddenly shots ring out from the darkened bend of the hall. The sound causes Griffin to loosen his grip, so Wylie tears himself free, taking off in the opposite direction to his classmates, who have all charged headlong towards the SWAT team staging the drill. Leaving the others to take on their mock school shooters, Wylie heads for the stairs, mindful not to trip over the volunteers who lay sprawled on the floor, smeared in fake blood, playing dead. If a student gets hit by a rubber buckshot during the shooter drill, they are supposed to drop down to the ground and hold a corpse pose until the demo is over. One time in sophomore year, Wylie got the idea to fake being shot, thinking it might be the easier way out. He hadn't realized just how many kids would trample over a fallen classmate as they fled or fought their way towards the evacuation points.

He is a few paces from the stairwell when a door opens to his right and a flashbang is lobbed out onto the floor, landing not far from his feet. He staggers back as the blast stuns his ears, leaving him half deaf and disorientated. He almost loses his footing, but rights himself against a wall of lockers to his left. A smoke bomb is thrown next, filling the hall with thick yellow clouds. Every drill day there's some kid who smuggles in fireworks. Wylie coughs and splutters for breath, retreating the same way that he came.

He comes to a door with its blinds down and tries its handle. When it won't budge, he tries knocking and calling out for help. He gets no reply. It's probably some freshman class who've barricaded themselves in and are sitting under desks with their hands over their ears. Wylie keeps moving, out of the smoke and away from the gunshots. Since the jokers with the pyrotechnics cut him off at the stairs, he makes for the boy's bathroom, figuring he can hide there until the SWAT team have moved onto the lower floors.

He's rounding the next bend when a bullet clips the side of his helmet, throwing him off balance. He crumples briefly to his knees before his instincts take over, running him the rest of the way to the bathroom. He rushes first to the window, looking over its ledge, considering if he could avoid death or injury from this height. He decides he's way too freaked out to risk a drop right now. Instead he locks himself inside the nearest cubicle, crouching on top of the broken toilet seat. He takes out his phone in a trembling hand.

"You…you still with me, Sam?"

A new message smashes its way into the sidebar of his stream.

I'm with you. I'm seeing everything. And I'm not the only one.

Before he can answer, a voice comes over the school's loudspeaker.

"Attention, all staff and students! This is no longer a drill. Repeat – not a drill! Reports of an armed student on campus. Continue to your nearest evacuation point."

Wylie's body goes numb. At first, he's sure he can't have heard right. He feels like he must be stuck in one of those nightmares that he's been having all week. Then he reaches up to his helmet and runs a finger over the deep graze in its side. A graze that could only have been made by a bullet. By a weapon not loaded with rubber or paint.

Did they just say there's a real gunman? Did they just –

Wylie's eyes blur with panicked tears. If there's an actual school shooter out there and if they're the one who just fired on him, they may still be nearby. And how are the SWAT team or the gun jocks going to know which kid has brought a real gun to this drill? How will they tell the bad guys with guns from the good guys with guns? The true danger from the fake? How's he going to get out of here alive? Wylie's shoulders slump and his backpack slides down his arm, weighing heavy on the crook of his elbow.

He frowns, eyes flicking down. Why's his bag so heavy?

Wylie places it on the toilet seat between his splayed knees and teases back its zipper. He peers into its dark folds. He sees the glint of gun metal between his books and then drops the bag on the floor like it's on fire. They've planted a weapon on him. Cooper and Griffin, when they snatched his bag in the library, they must have. And it only takes Wylie another second longer to come to another heart-stopping realisation.

The loudspeaker announcement. The report of an armed student on campus. What if that student is him? What if they've set him up as the bad guy this school's been waiting to take down? What if they've turned him from a lamb into a lone wolf?

Wylie hears the door creak, hears footsteps entering.

He tries not to breathe. He stares at his bag on the floor, the barrel of the gun still peeking from its folds. When his mom's boyfriend Larry had forced him to go along to the shooting range that one time, he…he hadn't actually been a bad shot.

"We know you're in here!" a voice calls from across the room. "Best show yourself or we're going to have to plug holes in all of these stall doors."

It's Cooper speaking, Griffin's sniggering laugh at his side. If this is no longer a drill, then the glass cabinets will have shattered, and they'll be armed students too. So he's facing a shootout of two against one. Only Wylie doesn't want to shoot at all. He wants the coast, and his college placement, and the permanent silence of gunfire.

He wants Sam. More than anything he wants Sam.

He looks down at his phone. She's still with him.

Wylie, your face. What's going on? What's happening?

He's still holding his breath as his sweaty thumbs type.

They got me trapped. And they planted a gun in my bag.

Wylie's about to add that he doesn't know what to do. What should he do?! But there's already a flurry of comments appearing alongside his stream. Comments saying not to touch the gun. Not to give them his fingerprints. Not to play their game.

Wylie yelps as a bullet is fired off. A real bullet that lodges itself in the ceiling above his head. A little rain of plaster crumbles down on him. He guesses this is the warning shot. He guesses they know exactly which stall he's hiding in now.

"*Yeah*! That's right! We're going to light you up, libtard!"

"Griff, *cool it!*" he hears Cooper snarl, suddenly not sounding pleased with his trigger-happy friend. "You high or something? Get out of here! I'll handle it."

His bullies argue amongst themselves, lowering their voices to whispers. A few seconds later he hears one of them spitting, then a loud slam of the door.

"Last chance!" the voice comes again. Cooper's voice, now sounding rattled. "Put your weapon down on the floor and come out with your hands up."

Wylie realises the flaw in this frame job. His bullies can't imagine that he hasn't taken their bait. That he hasn't accepted the gun as his sole means of fighting back. Cooper doesn't realise Wylie is already holding the thing that can best protect him.

I love you, he types to Sam and the others watching his stream.

Wylie slides back the lock and steps out from the cubicle, his phone thrust out in front of him, still streaming. Cooper's eyes widen on seeing the device, but he keeps his gun aimed steady. Wylie lifts his free hand up in the air, making it clear that it's empty. Cooper still doesn't lower his shooting arm. Wylie doesn't lower his either.

They both have the power to end each other right now. Call it a stalemate or mutually assured destruction, it's enough to freeze the air around them.

"I got separated from my class," Wylie says, forcing his voice to keep calm and civil. "I need to get to an evacuation point. Will you help me?"

Coop holds his stare, his cheeks burning red.

Slowly, grudgingly, they share a nod.

Chester author **Kell Cowley** wrote and illustrated her first novel at age eight, telling the story of a runaway radish escaping from a salad bowl to explore the far reaches of the vegetable garden. She has been perplexing her friends and family with her weird stories ever since. She holds a BA in Performance Writing from the wildly experimental Dartington College of Arts, won a novelist's apprenticeship with the Adventures in Fiction development scheme and was a prize-winning finalist in the international cli-fi competition for the 'Everything Change' anthology. When she occasionally closes her laptop or latest reading obsession to spend time in the real world, she will likely be found shambolically running a school library, attempting to act in local plays or eco-warrioring her way towards the apocalypse.

Reach Out And Touch Faith

K.C. Finn

"Is the coffee made yet?"

Isla shook her head. "No, Madam."

"Well then?"

The woman snapped her fingers three times, and every snap made Isla's ears twitch. She crossed the pristine kitchen to the automated barista, watching the bar slowly fill to green. It wasn't her fault that the bot hadn't finished producing the morning macchiato, but Madam didn't see it that way. Someone had to load and program the Coffee Gourmet 4050, after all. And Isla's fingers were never quite fast enough for the Madam's morning routine.

She seemed to be rising earlier and earlier these days, clinging to the breakfast bar with her e-cig in one manicured hand as the other waved to and fro to direct Isla's chores for the morning. As if the ever-growing, ever-glowing to do list inside her contact lenses didn't do enough of that. Isla forced her vision past the little glowing icon of the coffee cup that taunted her top-left periphery and bit her lip as she awaited the Gourmet's beep. When it came, three more snaps followed from the breakfast bar, and Isla poured the smooth roast with a shaky hand.

The Madam was hunched at the screen, a familiar sight for nearly-nine. News tickers flashed by on a display split four ways, the major channels competing for her fickle gaze. Isla loaded the coffee into the large woman's free hand, and spun on her heel to wipe up the residue over at the Gourmet. Inside her contact, the cup icon vanished, only to be replaced with the mop and bucket. Isla grimaced as she wiped a few stray foam bubbles off the bot's shiny chrome. She saw her own mouth twisting down in the shining reflection, and the grey sheen of her eyes where the contact screens masked their true colour. The grey marked her for what she was: a product of mistakes dearly made.

"Your dirty marks are everywhere in my kitchen, girl. Cleaning. Now."

She'd been hoping for a different task, one that would take her out of the kitchen before nine, but the Madam was in charge of the schedule, and her voice activated changes in every system which could hear it. The Industracleanse began to beep in the utility cupboard, filling one of its many tools with high grade toxic cleaning solutions and scalding water. Isla went to collect the pre-loaded mop, her shoulders rising to guard her ears. The pips were coming, and then the bright techno-jingle that Madam was waiting for. The climax of her morning ritual, and the moment which Isla had hated from the first day that she'd been sent to work for the woman who now owned her life.

Isla kept her head down as she handled the breakfast bar, taking the seats out beside the Madam with extreme caution. She dared not make a sound once the broadcast had begun, and even as she moved the first stool, the pips came blasting. The Madam tapped the screen, one broadcast now taking precedence, and she drew deep from her macchiato as she hunched her wide shoulders more and more towards the display. Isla chanced a glance at her face, lined and dusky without the sheen of the makeup she would put on later, before her business day truly began. For now, she could have been any other woman, hanging on the words that would follow the clanking, chittering music which hailed the onslaught of the most popular program in the nation.

"Welcome, welcome, morning viewers. I have been reading the codes just for you, and boy, do these codes have something to tell us."

He started each broadcast the same way, with that push on 'the codes' that the Madam mouthed along to. Isla's mother would be doing just the same back at the family home. For all the faults of her servitude, at least the Madam didn't expect Isla to actually watch the Techstrologist at work. Isla put the stools back, lifting them gently despite the ache in her arms. Her contact flashed with the coffee cup icon again. A second coffee was due by the end of the broadcast, which the Madam usually drank between her mutterings and decodings of the day's most pertinent message.

"Our midwestern viewers are going to experience a huge spike in energy today, and I'd advise you to handle it with caution. The codes can only provide the means to your success, and it's up to you to distribute the energy which they bestow wisely. Seek wisdom in the forces of science, and wisdom you shall have."

"Wisdom you shall have…"

The Madam repeated it, the nonsense hanging low on her breath. Isla raced back to the Gourmet to set up the second coffee, grateful for those few precious beeps that knocked the Techstrologist's voice out of her head whilst he rattled off a few other regions. Theirs always came last, central to the modern world of business as it was. Isla mopped around the machine to keep its hum in her head, but the Madam's repetitions grew more passionate with every mantra.

"Success is manifested in faith."

"The codes have all that we need, if we know where to look."

"We are all connected by the codes."

Isla clenched her teeth. She didn't want to be connected, not to this world or anyone in it. All the current system had ever brought her was separation, misery and loss. Since the Madam had bought out the zone, some three hundred people had been repurposed into new roles to fit with her corporate plan. The simple crafts that Isla's parents had once made, clothes and accessories with their own two hands, had been replaced by AI designs and autoweavers, which her parents had then been deemed too stupid to maintain or manage. Her father had started a movement, a rebellion against the Madam's machinations.

And people had started to listen. Too many people, with too many violent ideas about how to take her down. Isla's parents hadn't been quiet or careful about their desire for revolution, and the Madam had devised the perfect way to make them pay for their outlandish statements. Dark forces came, deep in the night, and Isla had awoken to a life of service in the townhouse, with nothing more than two uniforms to her name and the most highly automated home system she'd ever witnessed. She had tried to get out at first, and been sorely punished for her failures. No-one had ever come looking for her, and Isla suspected that, if her little family were all to keep their lives, then no-one ever would.

A year of these typical mornings had passed. A year of the Techstrologist feeding stories of yet more success and wealth to the already wealthy and successful. Isla gripped the chemical mop hard as she wended her way back around the breakfast bar. The screen was positioned so that the Madam could see it from anywhere in the kitchen, not that she ever moved when the precious young man with the codes and the answers was on screen. Isla mopped with fury, but her eyes kept flashing to his gaudy glory and wide grin.

The Techstrologist was eighteen at the most, a superstar coder who had risen to grace in as little time as Isla had fallen. He kept his name to himself, known only to those who worked closely with him from Pole News, the studio which had adopted him, and his viral ratings, with open arms and fat wallets. He was a slight figure who was always seated in a throne of metal, the camera never panning below the waist. The steady shot only ever changed to give those angular close-ups of his dark face, glittering with charm as he delivered his calm, confident words to the masses.

"Shush now, it's us."

Isla hadn't spoken, but the Madam often shushed imaginary noises that might interrupt her personal predictions for the northeast. Isla tried to mop slowly, but the Madam snapped three times, and she knew better than to move again. Keeping her face as level as she could manage, Isla held back her sigh, and focused once more on the screen.

"For my dear friends in the business capitals of the northeast, grave news awaits."

The Madam gripped her empty coffee cup so hard that her fingers changed colour.

On screen, the Techstrologist leaned forward on his throne, beckoning the camera to shift closer. His dark eyes shone, the briefest twitch appearing in his jaw. Isla frowned at the change in his mood, the hairs on her neck standing on end. She didn't believe a word of this nonsense about the codes and the connected world, but she'd be damned if he wasn't compelling when he drew people in.

"Act with caution in the coming hours, for the codes are disrupted in the strains of finance and health. A lunge in the direction of one may produce fallout in the other. Be vigilant. Never leave a single piece of data unprocessed."

The Madam nodded. *"Never leave a single piece of data unprocessed."*

She was up on her feet, angling as the Techstrologist said his goodbyes, and by the time his techno-jingle had played out, she had rounded the breakfast bar. Isla slipped out of her way, and the

Madam snapped her fingers over the gleam of the freshly-cleaned floor.

"Filthy. Do it again. And pause the coffee, I'll get it on the way out in twenty. I have calls to make."

The shift of instructions in Isla's contacts made her dizzy. She half-closed her eyes to the offending display, heading back to the Gourmet to cancel and reset the process. She was alone in the kitchen, the way she preferred it, but the tiny hairs on the back of her neck were still bolt upright. The Madam had never exited so quickly, or with such purpose. What could she possibly have gleaned from the Techstrologist's vague nonsense that would call her to action so sharply?

Isla chanced a glance back to the screen, the regional news now taking precedence. But the predictions from the codes were still running across the bottom of the ticker, highlighting the key mantras for success in the hours to come:

DISCOVERY. WISDOM. VIGILANCE. FAITH.

Isla turned the display off, cleaning the button afterwards as Madam would wish. She was finally able to let loose her sigh.

"What a load of shit."

⫸ ⫸ ⫸ ⫸ ⫸

"That was great, Gideon. Truly great. Viewers spiked right around northeast, very dramatic. Very-"

A hand was raised, and the man with the tablet fell silent. On his throne, the Techstrologist gave no other reply, his eyes focused on the team of assistants coming to lift him out of his seat. It was only when they had placed the young man back in his automated chair that Gideon let out a deep breath. His chest hammered, as it always did from the thrill of a live broadcast, and he needed a good long moment to bring his breathing back to normal. But he waved at the man with the tablet again, rolling his hand as the attendant nodded sharply.

"Uh, okay, so where was I? Ah, yes. We're getting sound reception back from internal home software. Ninety-six percent viewership repeating key mantras. Some background conversations, maybe sixteen, seventeen percent."

Gideon clucked at that. "Gotta get that noise down. My message ought to be received by the same reverent silence in which it's delivered."

"Yes, yes, of course, Sir." The attendant made a note. "We can restructure the intro from the newsroom to encourage that."

Gideon set the controls on his chair, and began to wind the familiar path around the studio. A phantom twitch made him glance to where his legs ought to have been, but he saw only the metal flooring racing by beneath his wheels. He crunched a fist, and was about to speak again when the clipboard man gave a small "oh".

"Oh?" Gideon studied the man skipping along at his side. "What's 'oh'?"

He saw the attendant's cheeks tense before the smile grew. "I'm sure it's nothing, Gideon, Sir."

The Techstrologist reached for the tablet himself, and he was never denied anything that he reached for at Pole News. The attendant's smile crashed back into the truth of his feelings as he handed it over. Gideon's nimble fingers scrolled the data for the anomaly, locating a minor alert which had flagged from the voice monitoring software.

Negative reaction: mild expletive.

Gideon raised a dark brow, tapping for more.

Capture: What a load of shit.

He scrolled for details, isolating the exact address, and the people who resided there. Gideon knew of Madam Larkin and her enormous successes in property development over the last few years. A quick cross-reference told him that repetitions of the mantras in her household matched the expected voice profile. But the second voice didn't. It wasn't a voice which had ever been registered on the system before. Gideon couldn't tell by the surface data where it had come from, and that set his teeth on edge. He stopped dead in his tracks, wheels whistling, and handed the tablet back to the attendant at his side.

"You'll have to excuse me from the post-show meeting. The codes are calling me."

Any mention of the c-word always inspired the same reaction from anyone at Pole News. The palms were raised, heads bowed as Gideon wheeled on amongst them, parting the tide of the cloying masses. Sometimes their total obedience gave him a flat feeling in his gut, but it was a necessary irritation to ensure that his plans were always carried out. He was their guru, the keeper of the mysteries, and so long as they continued to believe that, he had free reign to do whatever he wanted with the enormous broadcast capabilities of the nation's premier news station.

He reached his dressing room with little interruption, securing the door behind him with the click of a button on the arm of his chair. It was only then that Gideon reached for the phantom ache in the legs that he no longer possessed, rubbing the stubs under his tailored half-trousers and willing the sensation to pass. It had been four long years since he'd lost them, when he was quite literally torn in two by a bullet train that jumped the track and careened into the platform at New Grand Central. Other people had lost their lives entirely that day, but Gideon's had only truly begun.

The article remained taped to the mirror of his dressing room to this day, bearing the ominous headline **TEENAGE BOY PREDICTS RAIL DISASTER AND LOSS OF LIMBS.** As Gideon wheeled himself to the mirror, he let his eyes flicker over the image of his younger self, sitting in a hospital wheelchair, shaking hands with the mayor. It had been an offhanded comment in a video he'd been making at the station, bored whilst waiting for the train. But word had spread, and those precious few seconds of him predicting the disaster before it happened had orbited the globe, racking up millions of views before the tidal wave of fame came rocketing back to him.

It was a funny thing, the nature of faith. How belief had swelled in an ominous tide of whispers and fascination, the technological world coming together with awestruck emojis and viral hearts. Gideon had often wondered how the old religions managed it, when word was so slow to spread, and missionaries took so very long to find their way to the farthest reaches of the globe. But he had to suppose that the feeling people got when they saw his video was the same as they'd had hearing the leaders of old speak, and reading the words they proclaimed had come from some unknown power or other. Technology had simply sped everything up, just the way it should.

They had asked him how he knew, and Gideon hadn't wasted any time in making up a story to go with his accidental rise to fame. His eyes landed on the quote at the foot of the article: *The codes know all.* And so it had begun, his great ascension through cable talk shows and late night chatter, right up to the national news. And along with it, backlit late into the night by the screens from which he drank his information, Gideon had learned to speak a language that the world understood. And to program another, that nobody else could.

The mirror parted with the click of another button. Gideon had installed the partition himself, the place where the polished glass gently slid away, revealing a series of monitors behind it. Nobody was permitted into the room without his company, and so he had worked tirelessly to develop the perfect setup which he could connect to the processors and drives built into his chair. He was, quite literally, a mobile network, and the screens came to life with the sound of his voice as the chair gave a hum beneath him.

"Pole News Security Footage."

CCTV appeared across four of the six screens, the others filled with data on incomings and outgoings at the pass gate. Gideon studied the trends, finding nothing unusual for the day of the week. He did, however, catch one of the catering girls disappearing into a store closet, the assistant director for the weather report locked in a tight embrace as she too went in after her. Gideon smiled with a warmth that slithered down his throat and coated his heart. That would be useful at a later time. He clipped the footage and made some notes to transfer into his data bank, then he flexed his arms and stretched his muscles out. Now, for the serious business.

"Madam Ernestine Larkin — source address and full household."

The screens flickered through processing, and Gideon's warmth faded off. There was no record at all of anyone else being present at the Madam's townhouse. She was some three thousand miles away from Gideon's sunny studio, so it wasn't like he could just casually pop in to find out who else was there. Someone had to be, though, the voice profiles still didn't match, no matter how many pitch and noise permutations he ran. The second voice didn't match anyone else in his records either, which meant that a large number of the Madam's social circle were also out. Gideon rubbed his smooth chin, examining each screen until his eyes begged for rest.

And then he saw it.

A networked pair of contact lenses, the kind that servants wore in the most efficient households, so that the owners could update tasks by voice, even if they weren't in the same room as the staff. Madam Larkin had taken a servant, then, and forgotten to register her. Forgotten, or had other reasons for keeping her concealed, Gideon supposed. It was a grave oversight, given the

254

circumstances, but one which gave the young man a window. The warmth was back, spreading this time from his heart into his every muscle. He flexed, and the phantom twitches seemed warmer too.

"Patch full video and audio."

His earpiece crackled, and one of the data screens shifted to the live feed. He saw the furious mopping of a kitchen floor, and slowly, the under-breath grumbling of a young, female voice.

"Never leave data unprocessed. Unprocess this, bitch."

The girl mopped harder, slamming the edge against a polished kitchen cupboard with a slosh and a thud. Gideon traced through the data in the lens, reading the morning's basic chores, coffee orders and integrations with the household's many gadgets. He saw the Gourmet waiting for the girl's attention, and the Industracleanse notification, which held its standard safety warnings about handling toxic cleaning supplies. Then he pushed past her immediate tasks and into the coding of the program itself, where the voice recognition for her name would be stored. The name that the Madam used for her played in Gideon's ear, and he flexed his typing fingers, curling them like talons.

"Isla, Isla, Isla." He spoke to himself, his face warmed by the glow of the data, and the codes he knew so well. "Let's see if we can't change your thinking a little."

Some good old-fashioned aggression had transformed the kitchen into an even more pristine version of itself, every surface gleaming by the time the to-go coffee pinged in Isla's lens. She had cleaned down every finger-mark once the mop was back in the Industracleanse cradle, erasing her existence in the way that most pleased the Madam, and continuously reminded Isla that no-one would ever find her here, trapped in plain sight. Even the one-way windows of the house were a taunting reminder that whilst Isla might be able to see out, no-one else would ever gaze in. All anyone else knew of the Madam's life within her automated walls was what she chose to tell them. Another crock of nonsense that the willing were happy to swallow.

The Madam's clicking footsteps on the floorboards above told Isla that she had her heels on, ready to face the world outside. The girl quickly headed back to the Gourmet to fetch the cup, which had been sitting on the keep warm for so long that it was now scalding to hold the outer rim. But Isla's calloused hands took the heat, her feet picking carefully over the spotless floor to head out to the hallway. She would hand the Madam her drink on her way out, head bowed and silent, and then she would be free to go about the rest of her tasks in relative peace.

The macchiato smelled a little off. Isla took a sniff when she reached the foot of the entry stairs, her stomach lurching as she considered the possibility that the milk had curdled during the keep warm. But the Coffee Gourmet 4050 was supposed to be programmed to monitor that sort of thing. It was networked into the whole house, into the fridge where the milk was kept at a perfect temperature in its own compartment, and into the LAN that told it when it was likely to be needed at different times of the day.

Isla only had to do the dirty work of cleaning out the grounds and refilling the syrup pods, and of course, being there to hand over the coffee when Madam gave those three deafening snaps. It was 'a personal touch', according to the housing mogul, and that was what she'd missed ever so much in the days before Isla came to the townhouse. Sometimes, Isla had to wonder if the Madam even recalled that she had thieved her in the night, or whether she now thought of them in terms of some relationship.

"No, I want you to check the records again, Taylor." The Madam's heels grew louder, her voice carrying as she reached the top of the staircase. "Vigilance, today! There could be a mistake in the data, and I will not have it going into the final report without another check."

Isla rolled her eyes, but as the Madam took the first few steps down her grand entry staircase, the serving girl set her gaze to the floor. There was a flustered young woman on the other end of the line that crackled from the Madam's earpiece, and by the time the well-dressed woman had hit the bottom step, she cut it off with a sharp bark of orders.

"Do as I say, damn you!"

There was a beep as the line died, and Isla felt the macchiato being lifted out of her hand.

"Just what I needed. Today is going to be difficult... I can just feel it."

Isla nodded, and made to move away, but three distinct snaps held her in place. She heard the Madam take a deep gulp of her coffee, poised on the doorstep, and Isla winced as she turned back to face her. The milk was off, she knew it. The smell was all the more prominent now that the Madam was opening up the lid and taking a look inside.

"What the hell is this, girl? What have you done to my-"

The Madam hiccupped, one of those that brings vomit into your throat, and Isla crinkled her nose as the woman put a hand over her mouth. She grasped for her larynx, struggling to speak again. Her eyes grew wide as they fell on Isla. When the Madam spoke, her voice was raw and wild.

"*You... you're the data.*"

She clutched her stomach next, and Isla screamed as the woman convulsed with agony. The serving girl almost reached for her mistress, but what could she do? The Madam could no longer speak, all her cries burnt out of her bright red throat, her mouth foaming as she clawed at her own gut until her manicured nails snapped off, one by one. It was a frantic minute that seemed to echo for a lifetime, etching pained expressions and mortal motions into the dark recesses of Isla's mind.

And then, there was silence. Two women, one much older than the other, in the hallway of a high security house where every element of safety had been trusted to the machines which kept it running. The Madam's accusing look burned into Isla's head, but she knew that the blame could not possibly lie with her. She hadn't done anything except what the Madam had told her. Never stepped out of line when the Madam was within earshot. But now, that way of life was gone. It had died with all the swift severity of the woman who had caused it.

Madam Ernestine Larkin was dead at Isla's feet.

Reality came crashing back like a punch to the gut. Isla waited, her breathing sharp and stunted, but nothing changed. It wasn't possible. It wasn't real. Something was going to happen to make things right again. But Isla's contacts flashed red, the alerts and labels ripping past her vision with violent abandon.

VITALS OFFLINE. EMERGENCY SERVICES ALERTED.

Isla clutched at her chest, looking to and fro for some sign of what to do next. They would blame her for this, the police, and whoever else came. Whatever the accidental cause, the authorities would see nothing more than a disgruntled servant murdering their employer. She had no proof of anything, not even of why she was working here. The Madam had damned her, even from beyond the grave.

Isla's mind turned on a knife-edge, and her breathing slowed. There was no proof, sure. No proof of anything. Isla was unregistered. Stolen and blackmailed, silent and resigned. Nobody outside of the Madam and her presumably blackmailed parents knew that she was here. And she had spent the entire morning making everything spotless, removing every trace of her own dirty fingerprints from the scene, just as her mistress had commanded. The only traces of her proven existence were two work uniforms in the spare room, and her prints on the to-go cup.

The contacts would have to be dealt with too, but it was all simple enough, if she was quick about it. As the lens estimated the current minutes for an ambulance to reach the Madam in the heavy morning traffic, Isla found a series of words racing around her head.

Discovery.

Wisdom.

Vigilance.

Faith.

And from her lips, she whispered a borrowed idea.

"Never leave a single piece of data unprocessed."

From his mirrored room many miles away, Gideon watched the lenses fall, stamped out a second later under Isla's heel. His display turned black, and he disconnected from the feed, back into the Coffee Gourmet 4050 and the Industracleanse interfaces, ensuring that no one would ever discover that the mix up in their fluid distributions had been anything but accidental. Isla would vanish for now, but Gideon felt sure they would find one another again someday. He had heard her parting words, the hitch in her breath, the mantra repeating. His mantra. The Techstrologist smiled.

He'd make a believer of her yet.

K.C. Finn has been writing since 2011, at a time when extreme illness saw her trapped in the house with nothing but her imagination. Since then she's amassed a collection of stories, poems and novels spanning many genres, including fantasy, science fiction, gothic fiction, horror, paranormal and historical works. Her unique and diverse voice has won many awards, and she is both an Amazon and USA Today best-selling writer.

In her free time, K.C. is an eternal student, forever studying and learning more about the world. She travels whenever possible to explore new cultures and climates, and when she's at home she enjoys coaching writers of all ages with a story to tell. She also exercises her flair for the dramatic by directing, writing and occasionally acting in darkly humorous theatre productions in her hometown of Chester.

Check her out at KCFinn.com

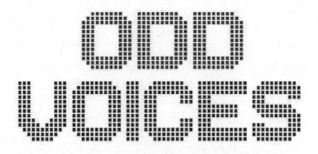

AN ANTHOLOGY OF NOT SO NORMAL NARRATORS

In every new story we pick up, we're seeking an exciting original voice. So why are there still voices we don't hear from nearly enough? Why are there characters that so rarely take centre stage? In this collection from Odd Voice Out press, we discover the stories of twelve teenagers who stand out from the crowd and who'll not easily be forgotten.

With settings that range from Scotland to Syria, Mexico to Mauritius, Africa to Russia, these stories take us to all corners of the globe and into the lives of young people with their own unique circumstances and perspectives. Characters dealing with issues of culture and class, exploring their sexuality and gender identity, or letting us into their experiences with illness, disability or neurodiversity. Their tales span all genres and can't be reduced to labels. These are stories about bending the rules and breaking the law. Stories of fighting for survival and finding your place in the world. Stories of family solidarity, unlikely friendships and aching first love told by teenagers who don't always fit in and aren't often heard.

With a foreword by award winning YA author Catherine Johnson, this anthology brings together the top ten stories of Odd Voice Out's 2019 Not So Normal Narrators contest, as well as bonus stories from in-house authors Kell Cowley and K.C. Finn.

MORE FROM ODD VOICE OUT

By Kell Cowley

One week before the Global Mandatory Hibernation and Flea
Wheeler will do anything to avoid a long winter underground. A
claustrophobic climate refugee who has been living rough on the
flooded streets of Manchester, Flea dreads the day she'll be forced
into shelter so a geoengineering experiment can attempt to reverse
the chaotic effects of global warming. Armed with nothing but her
stolen umbrella, Flea is on a mission to stay on the surface and
somehow survive the extreme weather.

'Shrinking Sinking Land' is a YA cli-fi story of survival, solidarity
and defiance in the face of environmental catastrophe for ages 14
and up.
Everything Change Climate Fiction Contest Runner Up (2016).
"Suspenseful…sharply well-written…and altogether a success."
Kim Stanley Robinson, *New York 2140*

SHADEBORN

THE BOOK OF SHADE

By K.C. Finn

Lily Coltrane's to-do list for starting university life is pretty simple:
1. Make friends
2. Meet a cute guy
3. Survive her first year in Modern History

In the little English town of Piketon this seems more than achievable, so much so that Lily even joins The Illustrious Minds Literary Society, an extra-curricular club that promises a truly unique social experience. What Lily doesn't bank on are the society's monthly visits to the mysterious Theatre Imaginique at the edge of town, a dark venue that houses the most obscure cavalcade of carnival performers she has ever laid eyes on.

Stranger still is the theatre's enigmatic proprietor, Lemarick Novel, a stupendous showman with a frosty wit who never seems to smile. How does he levitate with no sign of wires or mirrors? Why do the lightning bolts that shoot from his hands look so real? And why, of all the people in the theatre, do his pale eyes keep locking on Lily?

The answers to this and more lie buried in heritage and blood. The Book of Shade is opening, and Lily Coltrane will read it, whether she wants to or not.

The Vagabond Stage

By Kell Cowley

The West Country, England, 1599

Timony is a born actor before he even knows the meaning of the word. A restless farmhand with a yearning for the wider world, he is already seeking escape when he catches his first glimpse of a band of travelling players. His dramatic temperament makes an impression on the playwright, Makaydees, who takes him on as his new apprentice to enact the female roles. And Timony soon learns there will be worse things to brave than stepping on stage in a frock and wig.

The Vagabond Stage is a queer picaresque adventure novel exploring transgenderism in Tudor times aimed at ages fourteen and up.

FALLOW HEART

By K.C. Finn

When a gruesome murder spree leads to the door of a teenage loser, she is forced to face the reality that something demonic is growing inside her.

Fallow Heart is the story of Lorelai Blake, a self-conscious, overweight seventeen-year-old who discovers that a demon has pierced her heart, sparking an incredible transformation. Sleepwalking, fits of rage and impossible strength force Lori to accept that part of her is no longer human. It was hard enough fitting in before, and now that hurtful voice in her head has taken an even more sinister tone. Worse than this, bodies are being discovered. People in Chester are dying and they have only one connection: a nocturnal killer who savages its prey.

Fallow Heart is a tale of strength, suspicion and the supernatural for ages fourteen and up.

Printed in Great Britain
by Amazon

69740444R00153